Where the Butterflies Sleep

STEVE CAREY-WALTON

Where the Butterflies Sleep

To my wife Heejung.

Thank you for your enthusiasm and patience, as you must have heard this story a million times by now.

For sweetest things turn sourest by their deeds;
Lilies that fester smell far worse than weeds.

- William Shakespeare, Sonnet 94

1

Marigold's path to the phone was a line dance. Two steps forward, a side step, a twirl. Before the ringer lost its voice, she gathered her courage and picked up. "Hel—"

"Did you slip? You fall? What took so long?" Eliza's panic, hot and staticky, burst through the receiver. "You there, Goldie? I don't care how uncomfortable they feel or how much of a hassle they are to clean, you need—"

"I got my ears in." Marigold tapped her hearing aids. "Todd might try to reach me from the grave."

"Can you hear me rolling my eyes? I'm—"

Marigold pulled the phone from her ear to escape her sister's nagging. She paced back and forth, the phone cord restricting her like a leash, and perused the cards on the mantle. Handwriting was different when written in sympathy. More cursive than print. People wrote her name: Marigold, we are profoundly sorry for your loss. Marigold, we send you strength in these trying times.

"I'm here." She put the cards in a drawer. "I got distracted."

"Is it Alzheimer's?" Eliza said.

"Just dementia. You head out yet?"

"Roger's warming up the car."

"Leave in 10. I need more time to get ready."

"Don't you dare get ready for him. He didn't deserve it in life. And he doesn't deserve it now."

"I need to brush my teeth."

"Expecting a smooch?"

"Only from you. See you soon, Lizzie."

Marigold avoided Todd's room as if police tape blocked it off. It was not a crime scene, but he did die there. His unseeing eyes glued to afternoon game shows, a handful of pills, his last meal, sitting in his shrunken stomach. She had known before the nurse confirmed it. She didn't hear him gasp for air once all morning.

In the foyer, she stepped around boxes containing his kitchen gizmos—the bagel guillotine, the sous vide vacuum sealer—and her sewing machine, paint sets, and ukulele, artifacts from her failed hobbies.

She trekked up the stairs and passed the gym, the office, and the other guest room. Would the new tenets turn these spaces into baby rooms? Or would teenagers string Christmas lights and tack band posters on the walls?

In the closet, she slid long, short, soft, and scratchy dresses across the rack, the hangers clinking. She picked a black one, as if she had a choice, and put pearls to her ears. Were they jewels of grief? She clipped them on and examined herself in the mirror. The mirror, which Todd had placed at that exact height and angle to capture the bed. He always had to see himself in action.

As she brushed her teeth, she counted the plastic pill packs, curled and dusty, stacked in the medicine cabinet. She considered throwing them away. Todd would never find them now anyway.

She looked out the bathroom window. A squirrel scuttled across the pool cover, already distorted by the day's heat. When Todd had got sick last year, Eliza told her to pave it over and put up an awning. She had a point. They built the pool to catch cannon balls and house games of Marco Polo, not to accommodate Todd's geriatric water aerobics.

She went into the office and fired up the computer. The desktop was of a lake in Vermont. The water reflected the yellows and reds of the surrounding forest. Follow-up emails from realtors crammed her inbox. Nothing from Wendy, her niece who lived and worked on the other side of the country. In her digital shopping carts were ice skates, beanies, and jackets stuffed with goose feathers. Typing with two fingers, she searched for homes in the counties she had memorized—Chintendon, Bennington, Orange.

The phone rang—two sharp rings before cutting out. Eliza and Roger were nearly there. Marigold turned off the computer, soothed the sides of her dress, and made her way to the kitchen. She took out a nutritional drink. Wendy had ordered her a case, saying it kept silver foxes sly. She finished half the bottle, the chocolate flavor mixing with the taste of minty toothpaste still on her palate.

2

Their Rav4 idled in the driveway. The hood was flecked with rust.

"Wait." Roger power walked toward the house. His stomach curved out like the backside of a spoon. He wore creased khakis, once white sneakers, and a community college polo he bought with his faculty discount.

Marigold remained on the welcome mat. With her teeth, she scraped the chocolate gunk off her tongue and swallowed it. Above her a wind chime jangled.

"Take my arm."

She slapped at his bicep. "I can manage one stair."

"How are you?"

"I—"

"Lawn's dead," Eliza said from the front seat. Her hair was the dark gray of elephant skin. On top she had on a lime green corduroy blazer and a wooden crucifix necklace. "Mulch is easier to maintain."

"Yes, Lizzie," Marigold said. "You've told me."

Roger opened the car door for her. "Watch your step."

"She's deaf, not blind," Eliza said.

"All buckled in?" Roger moved the gear shift and backed out into the street. His eyes lingered in the rearview mirror. "New earrings?"

Marigold smiled.

"You're not helping," Eliza said.

"She looks nice," he said.

"Of course she looks nice—she never had a kid to ruin her." She angled her voice toward her sister. "Don't put in work for him now. He's gone."

"Your condolences are greatly appreciated," Marigold said.

"Please. His own family hated him."

"You hate his family."

"Hate him. Hate his family. Hate the lot." Eliza fiddled with the air conditioner knobs.

"It's busted, dear," Roger said.

"I know. Let me futz with it." She rolled down the window. "Todd better not have any tricks in wait, I swear."

"Betty has it all taken care of," Marigold said.

"She better."

"I bet he took care of Wendy."

"Have you seen the will?"

"He might pay off her tuition. He paid off mine."

"Have you seen the will?"

"No, but—"

"Then don't get our hopes up."

Marigold turned her attention to the highway, to the cracks in the concrete, and the cars exiting off into Hillcrest and Normal Heights. For a time, 40-some-odd years ago now, everyone she knew lived off one of these exits. But then high school friends moved away for college and never returned, while others scrambled back from a semester on the East Coast, nursing frostnip.

But they had had a choice. Marigold wanted that. San Diego was her home, but there was nothing left to experience.

As a kid, how many times did she ride the convulsing roller coaster at Mission Beach or stroll through the museums in Balboa Park? During the summer, she and her sister bussed to La Jolla to people-watch. A sort of pilgrimage.

They idolized the grown-ups on dates—high-heeled women wearing linen pants and rose gold jewelry, their arms linked with men in Cuban collar shirts.

And when she was old enough to look enough to drink, how many pints did she put away in North Park dive bars? How many days of her life did she waste at the beach? The heat seeping into her bones, making them gelatinous, unusable. Naps restored their rigidity. How many hours did she spend sleeping under a thin blanket of sand?

And then she was married. They drove or, more often, were driven to La Jolla. Todd ordered her blouses and loungewear from Chanel and The Row. They rented out chic venues in Del Mar with ocean views worthy of the city's name to host parties after horse races and football games.

"Keep your eyes peeled," Roger said as they pulled into the parking structure.

"Go back." Eliza stuck her head out the window.

"Is there a spot?"

"Go back . . . More. More. Keep going . . . I said more."

Marigold lowered her head to give Roger a clear sightline.

"A car's coming," he said.

"That's Allan's Buick." Eliza smacked the dashboard. "Son of a beaver."

"Are you sure?"

"The dent I left is still there."

They climbed a ramp and found a parking space between two concrete pillars.

"What's Allan up to, Goldie?" Eliza said. "You didn't hear anything?"

"Todd hasn't spoken to his brother in years," Marigold said. She thanked Roger for opening the door for her.

"So why's he here?"

Marigold kept silent until the question became rhetorical.

Eliza led them in and out of the revolving door's orbit. Lawyers escorted clients through the lobby, dress shoes and heels clopping. Roger pressed the button, and they rode the elevator to the third floor.

Betty sat on a bench, twirling her white curls. Above her head was the goddess Minerva enshrined on a plaque, the Great Seal of California.

"How thoughtful," Marigold said. "You didn't have to

meet us out here."

"Why aren't you in your office?" Eliza said.

"It's too small." Betty got up like a punch-drunk boxer. Even standing, she wasn't much taller than the bench.

"Expecting a crowd?" Roger said.

Eliza frowned. "Not now, Rog."

"I wish I had good news." Betty led them down a hallway. She looked down as she walked and didn't turn around until she came to a stop before a great door. "He added a codicil."

"I don't understand," Marigold said. Would she have to unpack the boxes and halt her search for a realtor?

"A letter." Betty reached for the door handle. "It changes the will."

3

"More people here than at the funeral," Roger said.

Todd's relatives slouched around a massive boardroom table, the back of their black-haired heads made them look like burnt matchsticks. Marigold recognized Jasmine, the daughter of Todd's cousin. Despite the 20-year age difference, Marigold would stay close and drink with her during family functions, navigating the minefield that was the Barton family.

Jasmine wore a short-sleeved floral print dress with shoulder pads that her sons were pounding with their little fists. Marigold smiled at her—a reflex. Even with the circumstances, she was happy to see her. But Jasmine didn't look up. She was engrossed in a one-way conversation with Todd's uncle, the only person there older than Marigold, who kept a protective hand atop the valve of his oxygen tank.

At the end of the room was a walnut desk. Completely bare. No computer, no lamp, no cup filled with pens. Behind the desk, a bookcase covered the wall from ceiling to floor.

"Ron's here," Roger said, waving to another cousin.

But Ron had his elfish, hairless face buried in a tablet

PC.

"I have to get someone," Betty said. "I'll be right back."

They found pockets of space to stand. No one budged to offer Marigold a seat. Instead, they spoke in the hush that accompanies the presence of books. Some had notepads. Children played tic-tac-toe on torn out pieces of paper.

"This is such manure." Eliza's body radiated anger, poisoning the air.

"We're not at Christmas dinner, dear." Roger put his arm around her, but she wriggled away. "This is the courthouse. We—"

"You all look comfortable," Eliza said to the table. A nephew scooted his chair back and began to stand. "Sit," Eliza said, and the boy obeyed like a dog. "Hey, Allan. Too traumatized for the funeral, but you made it today, huh? Brought the whole clan, I see. Great. We were due for a reunion."

Despite the gray fuzz on his scalp, Allan had the face of a smug teenager. He sat rigid, arms wrapped tight to his body as if wearing a straight jacket. Carol, his wife, groomed for the occasion in an oversized pantsuit, said something to him and he snickered. He flicked at the fake flower fastened to her headband. Veronica, his step-daughter, was slumped beside him, swiping at her phone and picking at the clumps in her mascara. "This is family business," Allan said. "Why are you here? What was your relationship to Todd anyway?"

"He's my bro—"

"Oh right. You were church buddies."

"His organs stopped working and his color changed." Eliza snagged Marigold by the elbow. "And Goldie was too weak, too distraught. So I fed him. I kept him company." She spoke faster. "I translated what the doctors said. Held his hand when he got the needles. And I vetted all his visitors. Didn't see you. Was that not family business?"

"He died alone, right?" Allan smirked. "What kind of man dies alone in his own home?"

Eliza was winding up for another retort when Carol stood and tossed a leg over Allan.

He grabbed his wife. "Where you going?"

She untangled herself from him and came to where Eliza, Marigold, and Roger were.

"What's he up to?" Eliza took off her blazer and gave it to her husband to hold.

"He collects the lint from his belly button and makes

me knit socks." Carol wasn't smiling. "He's here to recoup his father's inheritance."

"These aren't cans and bottles to be redeemed."

"I don't listen to him, and he don't listen to me." She shrugged. "A therapist wouldn't prescribe it, but it works."

While waiting for Betty to return, Eliza and Carol reminisced about their pickleball days. Together, they had formed a fearsome doubles pairing, dominating the local ladies circuit until Carol tripped lunging for a drop shot and collided with the net post. On cue, Carol chuckled at the memory and rolled up her pant leg, exposing a short zipper of a scar that bisected her knee.

The doors opened.

Betty whizzed past them and stood flush against the bookcase.

Carol threw a half-grin at Marigold. "Good luck today."

"Thank you," Marigold said, but her words went unheard, drowned out by a loud rattling.

Heads turned toward the door, toward the sound, as if tracking a hard-hit baseball down the line.

A man entered the room pulling something behind him. His mustache matched his eyebrows—thin and crescent-shaped. His upturned collar nipped at his ears. Dark sunglasses hung from the neck of his dress shirt, the exaggerated V revealing a Mardi Gras-amount of cleavage.

Marigold pressed herself onto her tip-toes, but Roger obstructed her view. The rattling grew louder, nearer. The in-laws cleared a path for him. She shuffled her feet, line dancing again, and moved her head in all directions for a peek, a glimpse of . . .

A cooler—more vehicle than camping companion. It glided on heavy-duty wheels. Enough cup holders for a family of six.

The man hefted it onto the desk and unsnapped the lid. Out came smaller coolers of varying sizes. He arranged them in order of ascending height like a dismantled Russian nesting doll.

"Dearly beloved, we are gathered here today to . . . just kidding." The man smiled and ran a hand over his iron-spiked hair. Confused faces spread across the room. "That's usually money." He opened his bag and fanned himself with a file folder. "Anyway. I'm Brad Mayer, Todd's lawyer and executor of his will."

The room exploded in noise.

"You said Betty had this under control." Eliza was nearly licking her hearing aid. "Did you know about this?"

Marigold's throat tightened. "How could I know?"

"Speak up. I can't—"

"First." Brad raised his voice over the cackle of conversation. "I want to give my condolences to Maryann."

Betty grabbed him by his shoulder and hissed into his ear.

"An apology," Brad said, "to Mrs. Barton." He tugged at his necktie.

Marigold imagined it as a noose and waited for the floor to fall away, leaving his legs writhing in the air.

"Mrs. Marigold Barton." A glob of sweat traced his forehead vein and inundated his eyebrow. "And a special thanks to Betty here. She's taken the ball 99 yards." He tucked an imaginary football to his chest and pretended to stride down the sidelines. "I'm just here to punch it in and do a little touchdown dance." He spiked the ball and twisted his hips.

Roger pinched the bridge of his nose. "Is this a stand-up routine?"

"I also want to take this chance," Betty said. Her head came up to Brad's elbow. "To offer my condolences to the family. And especially to Marigold, who has handled this tumultuous time with a grace that few possess."

Brad clapped.

"Please," Betty said. "The will."

He cleared his throat. "This is the last Will and Testament of Toddrick Joaquin Barton."

He held a single page. Scrap paper fit for doodles and grocery lists. The house, cars, the accounts, the summer cabin in Lake Arrowhead. Their futures all on this paper.

"Mr. Barton requested I deliver this message in his voice. Despite my extensive improv background, he was adamant about rehearsals, going over movement and how to build the tension. Rudimentary skills, really. But still, it took quite a few readings to satisfy Mr. Barton. Such a meticulous man, even in his weakened—"

"Bradley," Betty said. "These are busy people."

"Right." Brad held the will aloft and stared deeply at it as if he were Hamlet clutching Yorick's skull. "I'm dead now, I suppose. I'm sure that pleases most of you. For years, you tracked human-sized ticks into my parties and hiked up my booze bill." He mimicked the voice Todd had died with—raspy, singed with illness. "I didn't host any parties this year. And no one visited me. Were you finally waiting for invitations?" He flapped the paper until it stiffened. "It's okay. No hard feelings. I'm gone anyway. And don't worry, I'll be a lazy ghost; I won't haunt any of you.

"I can't wait actually. To die. I'm bored. Excitement is counting how many coughs it takes to draw blood. And wondering how the nurse's face will contort when she sees me.

"And yet . . . I'm not ready to disappear. Like all men, I want to exist forever. In some form. Like energy. Evidence of a man's existence is only what he leaves behind: his children. I bought baseball gloves and a tricycle. Picked out names. Nicknames. I poured my life into having a child.

"Unfortunately, the vessel I poured myself into was defective. I could have replaced her. Most said I should have. And I was lured. Rarely a week went by without a temptress offering me a trade: a taste of her ovaries for a taste of my lifestyle.

"I resisted like Jesus in the desert. But my faithfulness was unrewarded." He sighed. "And now my life is over, finished, left to be critiqued by lesser men. But if I had a child—a link connecting my life to future generations—I would still exist. Exist in memories. Exist as a character in family anecdotes. I would exist, at the very least, genetically.

"But that's intangible. Abstract poetry. We need a plan. We need legal process. So I, Toddrick Joaquin Barton, of San Diego, California, revoke my former Wills and Codicils and declare this to be my Last Will and Testament. I am married to Marigold Barton." Brad chewed his lip. And chewed. And chewed. Chewed like a toothless man working through a well-done steak. "The failure of this Will to provide any distribution to her is intentional. I direct that my residuary estate be distributed to my firstborn. The mother will act as guardian of the estate until the child reaches the age of majority. If no child is brought forth in a year from the reading of this codicil, the entirety of the estate will be donated to the Stand Up For Kids Charity."

The strength in Marigold's legs drained away and she needed the wall to keep upright.

"As the sole benefactor of my father's inheritance," Brad continued, "I know more than anyone the opportunities it provides. So now, I do invite you. Take my seed, my essence. Pour it into a serviceable vessel and make me exist."

Eliza buried her fingernails into Marigold's palm.

Brad took out an empty Petri dish and held it above his head. "Be fruitful and increase in number; fill the earth and subdue it. Rule over the fish in the sea and the birds in the sky and over every living creature that moves on the ground."

His face shone with perspiration. "There's a postscript," he said in his regular voice. "Step away from the others. And I shall tell you the mysteries of the kingdom. It is possible for you to reach it, but you will grieve a great deal." He returned the codicil to the file folder. When he was through, he turned to the audience, arms and smile wide, bending at the waist as if to bow.

"Brad," Betty said. "The coolers."

"Oh, right. There aren't enough for everyone, so"—he moved behind the desk—"it's first come first served."

Allan bolted up.

4

"Sinners burn in hell," Eliza said loud enough for everyone to hear.

But Allan was unaffected. He sauntered to the front like a bride down the aisle. Taking his time stroking each cooler's handle, he called out to his wife. "Babe, what's your favorite color? Babe?"

Carol didn't say anything.

"Fine. My favorite color is . . . This should do." He selected a red cooler.

"Please stay a bit longer," Brad said. "We have more instructions."

Allan turned away.

"Sir, I insist."

"I have good listening comprehension." Allan said. "Get the cooler. Knock someone up. And get the inheritance. Is there anything else to get?"

"Well." Brad turned to Betty. "Is there?"

"You're free to leave, sir," Betty said.

Allan signaled to his family and they met him at the

exit. The door closed behind them and for a moment . . . silence, stillness. Roger squeezed Marigold's shoulders. If she could move fast enough, she'd launch herself at the desk, tear up the codicil, and wield the coolers like clubs, bludgeoning everyone in the room.

The door ripped open. "It's empty." Allan charged in, the mouth of the cooler agape.

Brad lurched back. "They're sym-symbolic."

"Symbolic? What you trying to pull?"

"It's what the deceased—Toddrick—it's what Mr. Barton wanted."

"So where is it?" Allan swung the cooler once over his head like a lasso.

"I told you there were more instructions." Brad wiped the sweat from his neck. "But you wouldn't listen. Why wouldn't you listen?"

Betty placed a calming hand on Brad and stepped forward. "Did you find the paper inside?"

Allan recoiled. "I didn't see nothing."

"It should be taped to the bottom."

After a moment's search, he yanked out a white envelope.

"We're nearly through." She showed him to the chair behind the desk and faced the in-laws. "These fragile specimens won't survive in these traditional coolers. But inside is a set of instructions. First, call the number provided to reach the San Diego CryoBank. They will come to your residence and install a Cryo Magic 2000 freezer. Inside the freezer you will find six samples. In addition, you will receive a generous energy stipend and a personal consultant to help with specimen handling and the insemination process. Any other questions can be answered by your consultant. And as Bradly said, it's first come first served."

Five coolers remained.

A chair creaked. And then another. Muffled coughs peppered the air. In an instant, in-laws surged forward as if it were a Black Friday sale, felling chairs and stepping over crawling children. They jostled for position around the desk like skaters in a roller derby.

Marigold had fed these people, her supposed family, sent birthday checks to the kids and anniversary chocolates to the parents.

"Animals," Roger said. "Don't they know what happened to you?"

Marigold shielded her face. Her mind flooded with memories and flashed with images: meals in separate rooms; locked doors; Todd mounting her, his unblinking eyes trained on the mirror, at his thrusting reflection.

The first night she and Todd had made love—fucked, really, but he was dead and history was hers to warp—they didn't use a condom. "Trust me," he had said. "I don't want a child either." And when he did want a child, they fucked twice a day. She hugged her knees while Todd wiped himself and ordered her to lay still and let gravity do the work.

"Be strong, Goldie. For once." Eliza shook like boiling water. "Whatever you're feeling, swallow it." She seized Marigold's chin with both hands. "And swallow any tears before they fall."

Her tears ducts had been dry for years, but she nodded to her sister anyway.

It was over in less than a minute. Marigold counted three bloody lips. The oxygen tank rolled against the bookcase. Aunts swore at their husbands for being too slow, too old, and too weak.

Jasmine cradled the last cooler to her chest. She had lost an earring in the melee. Her two sons badgered her with questions, asking if the cooler was full of ice cream.

"Say, what did you think?" Brad said.

"Strange business," Jasmine said. "But Todd was a strange guy." She talked like a soldier on the battlefield, casting frosty glances to the surrounding in-laws. The smaller boy latched onto her leg.

"Not that." Brad played with the zipper of his bag. "Did you have a good time today?"

"Excuse me?"

"Were you entertained?"

"Entertained?"

"By my performance."

"What?"

"The reading of the will. I practiced a lot."

"Oh. Sure." She tried to shake her son loose. "I enjoyed . . . the . . . spectacle."

Brad beamed. "I got a set at the Mad House this weekend. You should come." He drew a flyer from his bag. "Find a babysitter and we can grab a drink afterward. My treat. The bartender gives his regulars a discount."

She stuffed the flyer in her kid's coat pocket. "My husband loves comedy. I'll pass it on."

Brad watched her limp off, her son an ankle weight. He offered the flyers to the straggling family members who left after checking under the desk once more for a cooler. "Quite the beauty, huh?" he said to Roger. An olive branch disguised as man talk. He petted the cooler for good measure. "She's coming to the beach with me this weekend."

"Should hose it off first," Roger said.

"Didn't you hear? There was nothing in the coolers. It's a symbol." Brad wheeled it out and shut the door.

Betty waved them over.

Roger and Marigold slithered into vacant seats.

"Where did you find him?" Roger asked.

"Todd called the firm," Betty said. "Requested a younger attorney."

"What did Todd promise you?" Eliza stood as if made of rebar. "How much was your cut?"

Betty ignored the accusation. "I wanted to steal the samples. Dump them in the desert to shrivel up and die. But I'm old. I'm the sheriff in No Country for Old Men." She massaged her temples. "Marigold, I'm so sorry. He was of sound mind when he switched lawyers."

"When did the switch happen?" Eliza said. "I took care of him every day. I would have known."

"Not every day. Not at the end."

"You mean the last month? I couldn't help him anymore. I'm a caregiver, not a nurse. I worked pro bono, I might add." Eliza knocked her knuckles against the tabletop. "But Goldie was always home. And she didn't see this . . . this coup coming. Right?"

Marigold nodded.

"He had us over while she was out," Betty said.

"Goldie doesn't go out," Eliza said.

"Groceries," Roger said. "I take her on Mondays. I maneuver the cart and lug the bags for her."

"There's delivery services for that. You don't need to be her hero."

His neck cords bulged. "Why should she stay at home? It's not a prison."

Eliza winced as if his voice had cracked. "Her mini-mansion is certainly not a prison. Anyway."—she turned to Betty—"So he masturbated every Monday?"

"He produced the samples years ago," Betty said.

Eliza tapped her crucifix against her top teeth. Her eyes were manic. "So this codicil—whatever it's called—it changed the will a lot?"

"I can't answer that."

"But you saw the original will?"

Betty's phone buzzed. "It was very . . . unfortunate for your family."

"What does that mean?"

"I have to go." She peeked at the screen and rose to her feet. "Got another case."

Marigold and Roger stood to say goodbye. They huddled together like a football team down by four touchdowns—quiet, eyes on their shoes—knowing whichever play they called next wasn't going to work. Betty hugged Marigold and whispered something in her ear.

"When can we expect your call?" Eliza said.

"I'll contact Marigold soon."

"Goldie only has a landline and, apparently, she's a socialite. She could miss it. Why don't you call me? Do you still have my—"

"I have your number. And Roger's. But I'll be calling Marigold."

5

"Todd loved the extra space." Marigold jabbed at the elevator button. "He lived in that office and bragged about our gym. We tried for a while, but gave up easily enough. I stopped drinking though. Tested my eggs. Anchored myself to the bed with my legs in the air. Held them up until they ached so I could absorb his—Oh. Sorry, Roger."

"We're family," he said.

"I'm not limber, but he read it in a magazine so—"

Lawyers filed in, tapping on their phones at stenographer speeds.

They stepped out of the elevator and exited the building. They walked by the flagpole, the California Grizzly bear dancing under a red star.

Eliza stormed ahead to the mouth of the parking structure and waited for them to catch up. "You said Wendy would be taken care of. Why'd you say that?"

"We've been generous over the years," Marigold said. "I hoped it would continue posthumously. She's the closest thing we have to a kid. We love her."

Forced to downshift to Marigold's pace, Eliza was antsy, a sports car in a parade. She zoomed forward, braked, and reversed to her sister. "Todd only loved himself."

"I love her. He knew that. Well, I thought he did."

They reached the car and got in.

"Are you going to call her?" Marigold said.

"Who?" Eliza shoved the seat belt into its buckle. "Wendy? Why? She knows he's dead."

"She called me after the funeral."

"So?"

"She was upset." Marigold leaned forward and spoke softer. "She felt left out."

"She did leave."

They drove away. The courthouse receded into the background. Roger turned to check his blind spot and winked his left and then his right eye—a signal to stand down.

"Okay." Marigold sank back into her seat. "Sorry, Lizzie."

"Just mind your business. You two may be close, but you're not her mother. Do you even know what she said to me? Before she abandoned us."

Marigold knew but said nothing.

"She said: Mother, when you die, I'm gonna burn you up. But I'm not gonna have you cremated. A charcoal grill and a chainsaw will do." Eliza's impersonation of her daughter sounded like a valley girl on meth. "I'll chuck whatever's left in a shoebox. I'll tell Dad and Aunt G, and if you had any friends, I'd tell them too. Tell them I scattered your remains off Potato Chip Rock. I'll tell them I recited scripture as the remnants of your soul soared in the wind to mix with the pollen to make new life. Doesn't that sound pretty? But really I'm gonna find a construction site near the border and dump your charred bits down a porta-potty."

"That's awful," Marigold said. With each iteration, her sister was becoming a better storyteller.

"She knows how precious my final wishes are." Eliza reclined the seat. "I wouldn't believe she was mine if I hadn't seen her pop out of me."

"Scenic route?" Roger piped in. "It's almost sunset."

"Go by the boardwalk." She caught his wrist. "And keep the radio off. I want to hear the ocean, not the same light rock we've been listening to for decades."

They settled into silence and drove by the beach. Surfers made for their cars, boards tucked under their arms, wetsuits unzipped, looking like half-peeled bananas. Small plates and wine glasses and highballs cluttered patio tables. On sand-dusted paths, cyclists weaved around kissing couples posing for pictures before backgrounds of pier, sun, and surf. Eliza's breathing—slow, but moving—matched the traffic. Her head lolled against the window. Marigold and Roger exchanged clandestine glances in the rearview mirror.

They turned east. The sun trailed them, until it tripped, fell, and disappeared.

Roger helped Marigold from the car.

"Goldie." Eliza rubbed her eyes. "Don't unplug your phone."

The house was the closed mouth of an animal, the boxes the hungry teeth. Marigold cranked the dimmer switch and gathered the remotes. Pointing and pressing, she turned on the electric fireplace and flipped the TV to a jazz concert. Overstimulated, she dug in a drawer for a lighter. Using both hands, she lit a stress-reducing candle. The cinnamon smoke got in her eyes, but still she couldn't cry.

She grabbed the phone by its neck and interrogated it. What did Wendy eat for lunch? Was there drama at work? Was she seeing a boy?

But she calculated the time change. Friday night in

New York. Wendy was sipping a martini at a rooftop bar in Manhattan or sharing a pepperoni pie with friends. No time for a chat with her fossilized aunt. Marigold would wait, as usual, for Wendy to call. If she had learned anything from her niece, it was to have appropriate expectations. No point in setting a schedule. Wendy called when she wanted: to vent about her roommate; gab about her latest East Coast adventure; or if she was bored on a date. To Marigold it was all, of course, trivial. But Wendy's intense innocence gave every event in her life magnitude. Even if only vicariously, it gave Marigold something to care about. And she needed something like that now.

Marigold unzipped her dress. Her balled-up socks, flung toward the couch, resembled argyle rodents. Sitting, she scanned her feet, cracked like sun-dried mud. Sacks of skin kept her calf muscles from slipping off the bone. Ashy knees. Blue veins careened across her thighs like lines on a road map. Her fingers reached under her ribcage, trying to grip a hunk of bone and break it off.

Her plans had reversed. The house would leave her. What had she done wrong? She had waited. Mouth muzzled and emotions regulated, she had waited. She even discarded thoughts that didn't serve her. For years she refused to dwell on the present, knowing it would engulf her like quicksand. Instead, she focused on the future. And that future was here.

She had done everything right and it was finally her turn. But the game of Life skipped over her.

Would she live the rest of her days at Eliza's, in Wendy's old room? What would even be the point? Like the ukulele she had packed away, all she had was sentimental value, which depreciated every day.

She slapped herself across the cheek and laughed.

Todd was gone and she was still here.

She was still here.

She recalled a line from a book and though she couldn't remember all the words, she sang it out loud, wrong lyrics and all.

"Only assholes feel sorry for themselves."

She counted to three and blew out the candle. After stretching, she pushed the boxes into a closet for the junk removal guys to take the next day. She climbed the stairs in her underwear and snuggled into a velour bathrobe.

***

Her dinner came from a box, cooked with microwaves. For dessert, she cracked open a bottle of sleeping pills. The capsules flooded her hand. She picked one—only one—and swallowed it dry.

On the man cave's TV, a saxophone player gyrated, possessed. The crowd encouraged the devil. The closed captions said [Music] and [Applause].

The sleeping pill's chemicals pulled at her eyelids, but she continued with the scheduled procedure, smoothing out a cloth on the coffee table. She popped her hearing aids out and cleaned them with a pick and brush, admiring the fire orange wax caked between the microphone and speaker. In the last few years, she had all but stopped wearing them at home, citing their discomfort and deterring conversation.

When she was through, she set them in their waterproof case, turned everything off, and headed for the stairs. A neighbor's car inched by the house, and she waited—training from years of fleeing the cave when Todd arrived.

When they were both home, she had played her own game of tag, maintaining a two-room buffer between her and her husband. If their paths crossed, she acted preoccupied with a jigsaw puzzle or a game of solitaire. Or she was reading. Always reading. Between new books, she'd re-read old books. Not so much reading, but coasting over the words. Her brain switched to autopilot as if driving down a familiar road. But at night, when she couldn't hide anymore, she slunk into bed, naked and drunk off vodka soda, because it was easier that way.

6

Marigold stumbled out of the sheets, eyes closed, tripping over herself to answer the phone.

"I had a dream," Eliza said. "The perfect plan. Get up. Put some coffee on, will you? See you soon, sis."

Sis?

She splashed water on her face and brought in the newspaper. Heat ricocheted off the asphalt. The lawn was brown and yellow like an overdone omelet. Neighborhood parents coated their kids in sunblock before they pedaled off to join their bicycle gangs. The adults loitered in a driveway. One mom conjured wet wipes from her purse that they used to clean their hands. Marigold stepped forward, the grass coarse underfoot, and watched them gossip. About what she didn't know.

She had always been received warmly at block parties. But she made sure to leave early, before the fireworks were lit or the piñata was smashed. It wasn't that they turned her out of the community; she just didn't have the qualifications. You can't get mad at the amusement park worker if you're too short to ride the roller coasters.

No one mentioned it. But they didn't have to. Marigold felt the tension on her morning walks juxtaposed against their morning rat race. Parents shouted with tired voices. High schoolers hauled spine-curving backpacks, pieces of toast or fruit in their mouths. Moms carried slow-moving youngsters by the haunches of their jackets, buckling them into car seats. They were polite enough, sparing a second and half to clobber together a neighborly greeting for Marigold who, for her part, never slowed them down with small talk or gave sage advice about how the day's clothes should be laid out the night before to save precious time.

Sweat was forming beneath her bathrobe. Her feet itched. The parents were still talking.

Back inside, she plunged her hand into the bag of gleaming coffee beans, filled the grinder, and covered her ears while the beans screamed.

***

"Smells great." Eliza hugged Marigold. The embrace was zealous yet cold, as if from a robot programmed to hug. She slid a paper bag onto the dining room table. "We brought bagels."

"My sourdough's ready to be tested too." Roger presented a Ziploc bag how a graduate would show off their diploma. "Made it from scratch."

"Settle down." Eliza opened packages of sliced tomato

and red onion. "You didn't grow the wheat."

"Looks . . . healthy," Marigold said.

"The bread's riddled with tumors."

Roger poked at the loaf. "The lumps hold the flavor."

"I'm too old for a yeast infection," Eliza said.

"Once it's toasted and buttered—"

"The bagels, Rog. Thanks."

Marigold set the coffee mugs on the table. "So this dream?"

"First, we eat." Eliza plopped pickles on plates. She dipped a finger in the spilled pickle brine and licked it clean. "Soldiers need to be fed." She mixed sugar and soy into her coffee till it became a beige soup.

Roger and Marigold dribbled capers on their bagels, while Eliza subsisted off a single sliver of lox she borrowed— her word—from her husband. "Did you have enough, Goldie?"

"Stuffed," Marigold said.

This side of her sister had been dormant like those cicadas that emerge every 17 years. As kids, Eliza had two voices: a phone voice that sang, "May I ask who's calling?" and another with a bloodied edge she used on her family. When their parents had friends over, she asked pertinent questions and gave specific compliments, her posture beauty pageant-immaculate. She was faking it of course—Eliza didn't care where these guests grew up and for every compliment, she had a better insult—but Marigold was roped in, complicit. Worse than playing along would be to rat her out.

"Ears in?" Eliza said.

"Locked and loaded. What's the plan?"

"Remember playing baseball as kids?"

"We never played baseball."

"Our version. With tennis rackets and dragonflies."

"I can't remember."

"At the old house. Before dad died." Eliza sipped her coffee. "We killed all types of bugs, but dragonflies were the biggest and the most satisfying. I'd whack one good and tear the wings and we'd fight over who got to pop the head off."

Marigold had drowned ants in dish soap—a peaceful death—but her sister had been the one to smash dragonflies and beetles with rocks and flip flops. "Are we going to decapitate Allan?"

"It's much simpler. We destroy the samples."

"Like insects?"

Nodding, she opened her pocketbook. "I couldn't sleep last night. Justice is a natural stimulant." She pulled out a piece of paper with phone numbers and names written in cursive. "I went through my address book and made a list of everyone who took a cooler. It's all prioritized." Her finger ran over the names highlighted in yellow.

"So." Roger scanned the paper. "We destroy the samples and then what? How does Marigold get the actual inheritance?"

"My subconscious will figure it out later. For now, we get rid of the samples."

"Okay."

"What?"

"Nothing."

"Do you have a better idea?"

"I didn't say anything."

"You don't have to talk for me to know what you're

thinking."

"We should call—"

"I spoke to Carol. Her daughter is 19."

"She called you?"

"Allan's not waiting for an appointment at the clinic. He's weaponizing a turkey baster as we speak. He'll steal your home, Goldie, and leave you starving on the street."

"I'm imagining whack-a-mole," Marigold said, "with machetes and crowbars."

Eliza laughed. "Those are options."

"But." Roger waded back into the conversation unsteadily. "This would be illegal."

"What's the crime? Murder?"

"Destruction of property?"

"What Todd did was legal, but it's not right."

"How about Betty?" His eyes rallied back and forth between his wife and sister-in-law. "We should call her."

"This happened on her watch. She can't help us. We have to do this ourselves."

"This is crazy. Marigold can live with us."

"That's not the point." Eliza hurled the paper bag, damp with salmon juice, at him. It fluttered and landed on the table, slightly torn from flight. "You're so quick to open the door for her and to carry her bags, but now, when she needs you, when she needs us, you won't fight for her?"

Roger went to the trash can and threw out the bag. He hovered over the succulents in the bay window and touched their leaves. "You really want to do this, Marigold?"

"You really want to do this, Marigold?" Eliza said.

"I don't sound like that."

"I got your lines right at least."

They stared at each other. Marigold looked out the window, at the pool. Would this be her life? Roger and Eliza arguing about her future like she was their sulky teenager.

Roger blinked first. "Why does it always come back to this? We weren't ready. It was an accident."

"It was a miracle."

"Yes. Without a doubt." He sat. "We know that now. But we were so young." His voice slowed and softened. "We weren't even married."

"So that's why you married me?"

"Of course not." He took a breath. "But it wasn't part of our plan."

"Our plan?" Eliza spat fire. "Our plan was for you to get your master's so you—"

"You told me to go back to school."

"—could get a better job or work for your father, not to become a freaking teacher. At a community college."

Roger bumbled and spewed like a blender with its top off.

Now this was her sister. It wasn't the first or the fifth time Eliza had unleashed this weapon of mass destruction. But the machine-gun speed of her words made it seem as if she practiced the speech every morning in the shower.

"I made that decision. The right decision." Eliza pounded her chest. "And Goldie will make this decision. And you can join or not."

"Okay." Roger rubbed his chin. "Marigold, what do you think?"

"Sounds fun," Marigold said.

"Yeah?"

"Yes." Did she have a better option?

"Okay." He slumped in his chair. "This will be easy. Easy as jumping into water without getting wet."

"Great," Eliza said. "Who needs more coffee?"

7

Roger trudged to the bathroom and ran the faucet for a long time. He returned with damp eyebrows.

Eliza smiled at him. "You look like you licked the toilet bowl."

"I'm fine," he said. Steam wafted from his replenished cup.

"Are office hours in session, professor?"

"How do we do this?"

"We have to play to our strengths." Eliza faced her sister. "And your greatest strength is your weakness."

"Thanks, Lizzie."

"You'll be our Trojan horse. You sneak us in. And we burn and pillage."

"I get it."

"Good. Let's start."

"Now?"

"We have sperm banks to call." Eliza entered a number and shoved the ringing phone into her sister's hand.

Marigold held it like it was a grenade with the pin pulled. "What do I say? I have no claim to the samples."

"You're a heartbroken widow. Desperate to conceive. Searching for your late husband's specimens."

"San Diego Cryobank. This is customer success agent Angela speaking." The woman sounded like a friendly flight attendant. "How may I help you?"

"Hello. I'm calling about my husband's samples. Do you have any? I beg your pardon. Is there any extra? . . . Marigold Barton. No. Oh. Ohhh. I see. His name. He recently died, so I'm a bit . . . because we always wanted a— Toddrick Barton. He disliked his first name . . . Yes, I'd be delighted to answer some questions. Of course, I'll hold."

Eliza mouthed: Confirm the kill.

Marigold verified her identity and gave Todd's DOB and address. "His name's in the system, but you don't— could you repeat that for me, please?" She cradled the phone between shoulder and ear as if catching up with an old girlfriend. "No specimens on-site? So his file's empty? Nothing at all? You sure? Okay. Well. Please don't apologize. It's not your fault. You're doing your job. Have a . . . have a blessed day." Marigold hung up and gasped for air. She had talked all in one breath and her lungs were swollen.

Roger gave her a golf clap. "I didn't recognize you. You sounded so . . . old."

"Don't pop the champagne yet," Eliza said. "We have to call all the banks in the area." She punched in the next number. "We can't have his gunk swimming in San Diego, polluting our waterways."

"Let's do this outside," Roger said. "It's a beautiful day."

"You want another heat rash? Besides, I need you to go online and compile everything you can find on the"—she wrote it out—"Cryo Magic 2000. And get Goldie a glass of water while you're up."

Roger saluted.

"Not bad, sis," Eliza said. "But you need to be more efficient. And you need to be sadder. Lead with death. Always lead with death. Ready for round 2?"

The calls continued. They were seasoned relay runners, passing the phone back and forth like a baton. During intermissions, they tightened their game plan. Like a calculated chess player, Marigold knocked out her opponents with the same opening, the same order of moves. Roger returned with a stack of papers and refilled their water glasses.

Marigold extended her wrinkled hand. "I'm ready for

the next one."

"We're done." Eliza dropped the phone in her bag, sealing it shut with a rip of the zipper. "There isn't a drop left in the county. But you—"she flipped through the papers—"what'd you get me?"

"The user manual." Roger puffed out his chest. "All I did was search—"

Eliza grabbed him by the neck and kissed him. When she pulled away, his lips were still pursed.

Marigold busied herself with a long drink of water.

"We have a problem." Roger wiped his mouth. "The freezer has a passcode. Akin to a hotel safe."

Eliza studied a few pages, got up, and slung her purse over her shoulder. "Let's go."

"What about lunch?"

"I have too much to do." Eliza waved the thick manual. "You're not hungry are you, Goldie?"

Marigold shook her head, silent, unsure which voice would spill out.

"Rest up, sis. Give your ears a thorough cleaning. Too much semen talk for one day."

Marigold walked them to the door, going no further than the welcome mat, speckled with dirt and leaves.

"You're quite the voice actress." Eliza hopped in the car and rolled down the window. "But you'll be hitting the stage soon."

***

After they left, Marigold wrapped herself in her robe and sat on the bed. Fatigue spread from her buzzing throat to the rest of her body, her limbs heavy and tingling. But it was a good tired, as if she had spent the day at the beach.

The bed caught her fall. The phone was in reach—on the nightstand—but her words were raindrops trapped in a cloud. No chance of showers. She called anyway, content to listen to Wendy talk about her day, listen as if it were a lullaby. But she fell asleep to the ceaseless ringing.

8

In the bathroom, Marigold tried on different voices. She dropped and raised octaves. Stooped over, she flexed her blossoming hunchback.

After a week of experimentation, she had fine-tuned the crying recipe: 10 big yawns—hold the blinks—and a scroll through the mental Rolodex. More sweat than tears—moisture from exertion, not emotion—but her frown lines tightened and her eyes were fiery, colored in red.

***

The coffee pot was bubbling when Roger and Eliza arrived.

Roger peeked in the fridge and combed through the vegetable crisper.

"Hungry?" Marigold pulled out chairs for her guests.

"We need to go shopping."

"There's plenty in the pantry. Soup cans, bags of pasta, canola oil. I'm ready for the apocalypse."

"We have coffee. That's all we need." Eliza exchanged a stapled packet for a cup of joe. "And the script."

"I'm so ready," Marigold said, thumbing through the

pages.

Eliza brushed her sister's puffy eyelids. "What do you do if the husband answers?"

"Hang up."

"Which son do you proceed with?"

"I hang up on any male voice."

"What did they give at your wedding?"

"An acacia cutting board."

"And what does that mean to you?"

"The board is a metaphor for our relationship." She answered like a Jeopardy contestant mowing down a pet category. "Even after a period of disuse, I can take it out—no apologies, no excuses—and depend on it, as if no time has passed."

"That last line sings," Roger said.

"I can't believe you chose teaching over screenwriting," Eliza said.

"But the rest." He took the script and read the opener. "Does this need to be workshopped?"

"Let's find out," Marigold said. "Dial."

"Hold on," Eliza said. "Teams lose when players doubt the game plan." She brought the mug to her nose, breathed in the aroma, and said, "The lie is built on a foundation of truth. Jasmine will believe it because she treated Goldie the best over the years. But think about it. We're telling her she won the lottery. Right?"

Roger nodded.

"She'll believe it because she wants it to be true."

"Makes sense," he said.

"I'm calling." Eliza buried her teeth in her bottom lip and turned on the speaker phone.

With each ring, the juices in Marigold's stomach burbled up to her throat. For decades, silence had been her weapon. Attrition her strategy. But now she had to—

"Yes?" The voice on the other end was barbed, a deterrent to telemarketers.

"Jasmine?"

"You got me. What do you want?"

"It's Marigold. You have a minute?"

"Um."

"Marigold Barton."

"I know. How are you?"

"Doing better than Todd."

"That's . . . you still have my number?"

"I should have called more often."

"No, I—"

"Should have invited you to this house . . . while I could."

After a moment's pause, Jasmine said, "I'm sorry."

"You didn't kill him."

"We didn't go to the funeral and—"

"You have two boys. You're busy. I'm no mother, but I do understand."

"You're family. But at the courthouse. We . . . We were awful—"

"That's why I'm calling." Marigold made her voice Christmas carol cheery. "This house is too much for me. I'll break a hip on the stairs or drown in the pool. You know, I'm not allowed on the road anymore? It's a waste to own a car museum, don't you think?"

"I guess."

"I'm going to move in with my sister."

"That will be for the best."

Eliza pointed to the word "family" in the script.

"Of course I'm disappointed. But"—Marigold pushed away the papers; she had to improvise to make it real—"we bought this house because we wanted a family. Now, it's just me; less than what we started with. But this house was meant to have a family. And you know what, Jasmine?" She sniffled. "You have a family. You were always nice to me. I want you to have it."

"That's gracious of you." Static. The receiver passed from one ear to another. "But what about the codi-seal?"

"I've spoken to Betty, my attorney. It's possible."

"She said that?" Jasmine was breathless. "Should I get a lawyer?"

Eliza mouthed: slow down, but Marigold didn't need the coaching. "I'd rather not say over the phone."

"I'll swing by," Jasmine said. "The boys are out."

Eliza shook her head furiously, chanting no no no under her breath.

"That might look bad," Marigold said. "If it's not too much, can I come over?"

"You gonna taxi? I don't have time to pick you up and bring you all the way back."

"My brother-in-law will give me a ride."

"Does he know why you're meeting me?"

"I'll tell him I'm seeing a friend. For lunch?"

"Yeah, okay."

"He's got errands to run at the mall. You still live in Mission Valley?"

"Yeah."

"Not for long you do." She laughed.

They agreed to meet in an hour and hung up.

"It worked," Roger said.

Eliza punched him in the shoulder. "Of course it did." She pounded the table. "Incredible performance, Goldie. You—are—a—spider." She got up and poured herself another cup, the coffee a black waterfall. "Rog, go to the garage. Get everything ready."

He skipped out of the room.

Eliza stirred in milk, the spoon clanking against the mug. "Did you shower?"

"You told me not to," Marigold said.

"Stand. Spin. Hmm."

"What?"

"You look too put together."

Eliza went out to their car and returned with a shopping bag of clothes. In the bedroom, she dressed Marigold in a pair of faded slacks and a baggy blouse with a sauce stain near the collar, friendly fire from a tri-tip sandwich. "Hope you can stand wearing my rags for a while."

"They're nice. A bit . . . roomy, but nice."

"You could never lie." She unhooked her sister's necklace and removed her earrings. "Can you cry again?"

"Let's see." Marigold snatched a memory in arm's reach—her in-laws fighting over the coolers—and started yawning.

9

Eliza sat in the back of the RAV4 with her seatbelt undone. Her swirling fingers worked over Marigold's hair, creating snags and eddies. "You can't make a whole sundae in one scoop."

They exited the freeway.

"The priority is to keep your cover," Eliza said. "If you can't get the passcode, you can't get the passcode." She flicked strands of her sister's hair out the window. "But try to get the passcode."

"Uh-huh." Marigold grabbed the handle above the door.

"Let her do the talking." Her fingernails crept into her mouth. "And call twice. Leave a message to show you're committed."

"You're freaking her out," Roger said.

"She's fine. You're fine, right? You have been quiet."

"I'm getting into character," Marigold said.

"Such a thespian."

Roger pulled over. "We're here."

"Wait." Eliza crawled to the car floor.

"What are you doing?" Roger said.

"Jasmine could be spying on us."

"So?"

"I'm not supposed to be here."

"I'll call you." Marigold stepped out.

"You got everything?" Roger said. "For Plan B?"

She tapped her pocket. "I hope I got my motor skills."

"Just remember: lefty loosey."

She went to close the door.

"Hey," Roger said. "Whatever happens . . ."

Marigold followed his gaze, which landed on Eliza, taking cover under the seat.

"Never mind." He turned off the hazard lights. "I don't want to jinx you."

Marigold passed through the busted security gate. Rusty padlocks chained rusty beach cruisers to the courtyard fence. Topless Barbie dolls slept beside water guns for protection. Balconies were prison cells for potted plants, crusty beach towels, and cats with moth-eaten fur. On a first-floor patio, two skinny, shaggy headed shirtless men slobbered on a hookah hose and blew deformed smoke rings. The bass of their electronic music made the glass door vibrate.

The building had no elevator.

Marigold paused in the stairwell. Cigarette butts and bubble gum cud congregated in separate corners like cliques. She and Eliza had played rock-scissor-paper on stairs similar to these. Without the inheritance, could she even afford to live here? She tried to visualize success, but all that came to mind was Todd's smirk that meant I own you. You're mine.

***

Jasmine flung the door open and welcomed Marigold with a big hug. "You look . . ." She pointed to the stain on her shirt. " . . . hungry. Hope you're ready for tuna." With her Chargers shirt billowing, she showed her to the kitchen. Magnets from the Grand Canyon and Lake Tahoe and crooked pictures of her family playing mini-golf covered the refrigerator. Around the square table, the chair breeds varied in size, color, and shape.

"Cozy home." Marigold settled in the lone cushioned seat. "I'd love a tour."

"A verbal tour should do. There's the boys' room. Our

room. Bathroom. You came in through the living room and now you're in the kitchen. Mitch is so tall he can stand right . . . here and practically pivot into each room." From a shelf, she took out a red toaster and brought it and a bag of white bread into the bathroom. The toilet seat closed with a thump. "Most people don't have enough counter space," she said from the restroom. "We don't have enough outlets."

While Marigold chewed through the toilet-toasted bread and the celery and onion cemented in mayonnaise, Jasmine complained her youngest son was becoming a rambunctious fibber. After lunch, she boiled water for tea and packed the extra sandwiches into Tupperware, tinged orange with spaghetti sauce.

"Those for your boys?" Marigold silently yawned and stopped blinking.

"They're locusts when they get home from camp."

"They take the bus?"

"I pick them up. Soon actually." Jasmine slid two ashtrays onto the table, "The Peppermill Casino" etched on the sides in chipped lettering.

"Sorry, I don't smoke."

"From our honeymoon. In Reno." She poured hot water into two coffee-stained mugs. "Mitch swiped one from a blackjack table, and I nabbed this one from the penny slots. Exchanged them as wedding gifts."

"The Gift of the Magi." Marigold dragged the mug toward her. "But the opposite."

"The Magi?" She plopped her sopping tea bag into the ashtray. "I can't smoke anymore, but they're useful." She stole a sip and dunked the bag back into her mug. "It's not steep enough."

Marigold decided to launch her attack when the tea was ready. For now, she kept her head down and pawed at her eyes, thinking of her parents. How dad would always put toothpaste on mom's toothbrush. And how mom, whenever she went out, would leave a list of chores written on the back of a torn envelope.

The scent of ginger and lemon strengthened as the color of the tea deepened and yellowed. Marigold drank; the crisp heat warmed her throat. "I meant what I said on the phone."

"Can I ask a question?"

"Sure."

"The house has two living rooms, right?"

"Sure does."

"Okay. Good."

"Do you have any other questions?"

Jasmine strummed the string of her teabag. "Our law-yers will do the talking and paperwork, right?"

"We can talk a bit." Marigold took Jasmine's hand. "What do you want to know?"

"How many cars are there?"

"Enough for everyone in your family."

"I heard . . . Do you have an elevator?"

Marigold swallowed her laugh. "No, though I could use one."

"Is the pool in good shape? You don't seem like you use it since you said you were worried about drowning. My boys love to swim. But the ocean's too dangerous and the public pools got too many rules. It would keep them occupied. Plus, won't have to run the AC as much in the summer. Throw the kids in there and—"

"I have a pool guy." She held Jasmine's hand like an arachnophobe handling a tarantula. "There's a hot tub too."

"The boys will love it then."

"I hope so." Marigold gulped audibly. "I have something to ask you too. The day at the courthouse, you received a cooler."

"It was empty." She tried to pull her hand back, but Marigold had her by the wrist. "We didn't receive the samples for days."

"Samples? That's so cold. So . . . dead. No. No. No." On cue, tears came to her eyes. She covered her face. "They were a part of him. They were him."

"I, uh, never thought of it that way." Jasmine sounded unsure, as if speaking a language she hadn't used in years. "Hang on." She tore sheets of toilet paper from a roll on the counter. "You're right. It is . . . alive."

Marigold mopped up her tears with the translucent tissue. "Imagine if they were taken from you." She motioned to the photos on the fridge. "And all you had was . . . But I don't have anything."

"What about his stuff?" She pressed her fingers to the table, playing a complex piano chord, gathering bread crumbs and flicking them onto her plate.

"I have no claim to his possessions. Besides, those are

things. They aren't . . ."

"Alive?"

"Exactly."

Jasmine brought the plates to the sink, flipped on the faucet, and sprayed the dishes. "Would you like to see the samp—Would you like to see him?"

"I'd love that." Marigold smiled hideously; her left eye twitched.

The bedroom walls were blistered with water damage. On the nightstand was a miniature statue of Madonna del Parto—Our Lady of Childbirth. Marigold recognized it because her mother-in-law had put a prayer card of the Lady under her mattress.

"Don't mind the laundry. They're clean." Jasmine cleared space on the bed. "Just need to fold them."

Marigold sat next to a mound of blue dress shirts and neon vests with "Security" printed across the middle.

"Took forever to be able to sleep with the noise," Jasmine said.

"I don't hear anything."

"It's on a cycle. I swear it waits until I finish counting sheep to start whirring." Jasmine pulled the closet doors open and moved the hanging clothes to the side.

The silver machine rested on the floor. It had a vent in the corner; a cord stretched out the back. To the left and right of it were clogs and loose-laced work boots.

The user manual promised the passcode would be four digits. Marigold could remember four digits. Less than half her social security number. She scooted over for a better look and knocked a pair of boxer shorts to the floor. She bent down to snatch them up.

"Do me a favor?" Jasmine was on her knees, her elbow propped on the freezer. "Put my husband's boxers down and get the gloves in the top drawer of the dresser? The nurse said we'd suffer ice burn."

The knobs were missing from the drawer, so Marigold had to insert her fingers into the gap to slide it open.

"I only have the one pair they gave me," Jasmine said. "We'll split them."

Marigold wrestled the purple glove on, her eyes fixed on the number pad, which resembled the buttons on a microwave.

"I kept everything they sent me in there," she said.

"The instructions. The consultant's phone number. Did you see the box?"

"No."

"Check it out."

Marigold returned to the drawer and took a closer look. Pens. Faded documents. An old bra that opened at the front and a long thin box. "What is it?"

"Open it."

Inside was a tube in clear packaging. A syringe without the needle.

"It's an insemination kit," Jasmine said. "They showed us—well they didn't demonstrate—but they showed us how to use it. The end is supposed to resemble a pee hole."

Through the packaging, Marigold fingered the slit at the end of the tube. "It's so reali—"

Beep.

Beep.

Beep.

Beep.

Marigold turned. Smoke billowed from the open freezer.

"Oh, this is nothing," Jasmine said to Marigold's shocked expression. "When they brought him over in the liquid nitrogen tank, I lost my kids in the fog." She grabbed a sock and fanned away the smoke. "They think we're hoarding ice cream. I catch them snooping in here all the time, even though their daddy can't have dairy without shitting his pants."

"Kids." Marigold felt for the mini screwdriver tucked in her waistband. It dug into her thigh, but the wad of duct tape wrapped around the tip dulled the pain.

"I'm glad you called." Jasmine pinched a vial. The smoke was dissipating. "I'm too old to be surrogated and having a baby for money doesn't seem right."

Marigold accepted the vial, their gloved hands coming together, and cleared the condensation.

"You know, I like spending time with you," Jasmine said. "Near you, I feel closer to the life I wanted. Big house. No kids. My own free time."

Marigold put the vial against her heart. The icy bullet sent a chill through her body. "If I could, I'd trade it all for what you got."

Respecting the sanctity of the ritual, Jasmine bowed her head. But after a moment, she said, "It'll thaw. I have to put it back. Unless . . . you still ovulate." She giggled.

Marigold might have laughed along if she wasn't in character. "I swear it looks familiar." She titled the vial, but the substance didn't move. The swimmers were microscopic bugs trapped in amber. "Here."

The vial fell, broke. Crystal gravel scattered across the floor.

"My arthritis." Marigold gawked at her hands, at their betrayal.

Jasmine seized the sock on the dresser.

"No," Marigold said. "Damp dishcloth."

She darted for the kitchen.

Pouncing to the floor, her knees screaming, Marigold molested the machine. She followed the power cord to the outlet guard. One, two. Two screws just as the manual had said. From the kitchen, the sink ran and a rag snapped. She sat up straight and fumbled for the screwdriver. The tip nicked her abdomen. The floor vibrated with oncoming steps. She stashed the screwdriver inside a loafer and spun like a wobbling top to face the mess.

"Let me take care of that," Jasmine said with composure, a veteran of innumerable spills.

"I need to do it." Marigold was crying again.

"But there's glass."

"Please." She took the rag and punched the floor. "Todd, I'm so sorry."

"I'll"—Jasmine backed out of the room—"I'll let you be alone."

Marigold's vision was blurry. Her lower back burned. She wiped away the tears and glanced at the door—open a smidge—expecting to find Jasmine, phone to her ear, calling the police. Instead, she saw into the boys' room. Maniacally scribbled landscape drawings tacked on the wall.

Relax.

All the time in the world. If Jasmine returned, she would feel it through the floor first anyway, like an animal sensing an earthquake.

Focus.

She breathed deeply through her nose and braced her screwdriver hand.

Lefty loosey.

The new screws made for easy work. The plexiglass guard came off simply enough. With one pull, she unplugged the machine. Would Jasmine notice?

She cleaned the mess, wiping in broad strokes. She sheathed the screwdriver into her underwear's waistband, careful to first wrap the tip with the piece of duct tape. As if ending the show, she closed the curtain of pants and long jackets on the freezer. She snuck in the hallway and placed the guard and one screw on the boys' dresser.

"Where should I put this?" Marigold held the weighty rag, covered with the stray curlicues of body hair she'd moped off the floor.

"You can keep it." Jasmine wore sunglasses and a fanny pack. Her car keys were on the table. "If you want."

"No. Sorry. I haven't been myself."

"You're grieving. The trashcan's there."

Marigold disposed of the rag and washed up at the sink. "Could I use your phone to call Betty and let her know we're on the same page?"

"In the living room."

Marigold dialed Eliza's number. "No answer," she hollered back to Jasmine, who was leaning out of her chair, ears pricked. "I'll try again." From the window, she saw the RAV4 lurk into view. "Hey, Betty. It's Marigold Barton. Sorry to have missed you. I have news. Jasmine's on board. Call me at home and let's talk about the next phase. I'm eager to get this done as soon as possible. Goodbye."

***

Once on the freeway Eliza popped up from the floor. "Status report?"

"I destroyed one sample." Marigold flopped back against the headrest. "And unplugged the freezer."

She tapped Roger on the head. "Told you she could do it." Out came her crucifix and she peppered it with kisses. "Isn't this fun?"

"It'll be more fun if it works." Marigold's head throbbed. Only now did she realize how tense she had been. She had kept herself on for too long. She was overheated, bordering on malfunction. With an earthquake hand, she rolled down the window and used her palm to angle the wind into her face. "When will we know?"

"This Tuesday," Roger said. "Or next Tuesday."

"That's specific." The fresh air relaxed her.

"It's trash day."

***

They stopped at a Hawaiian restaurant for poke bowls. While their order was being prepared, Marigold went to a liquor store and bought a bottle of Riesling. Food, wine, and a movie in Todd's room.

A celebration.

The house wasn't any closer to being hers yet, but she had a tighter grip on it. And she'd never let go.

***

Roger left the engine running. "Be right back."

Eliza sucked the beans from an edamame pod and placed the spent shell in the cupholder. "Make your chivalry quick."

Roger and Marigold walked up the driveway to the house, their shoulders coming together every other step. Marigold unlocked the door. "Set those down." She took off her shoes and turned on the lights.

"Then you'll have to pick them up again."

"You're too much."

Their fingers touched as he passed her the food and wine bottle. She made sure not to watch him leave.

There was a message on the answering machine. Perfect timing. She could finally contribute to their conversations. She'd brag to her niece about her exploits at Jasmine's. Ham up how she destroyed the sample and disclose her plans to move to the East Coast so they'd be near each other. Wendy might cry from being so happy. She'll probably volunteer to be her soldier on the ground, relaying real estate information and calculating differences in cost of living.

But as she formed these thoughts, she heard Eliza reprimand her: Don't take the cake out while it's baking. Her sister was right, like always. Marigold would stay quiet until the news was good and final. Her hands full, she pressed the play button with the tip of her elbow.

"Hi, Goldie. Can I call you 'Goldie'? I know only your sister calls you that, but . . . after today, I feel like we're at that level. Don't you? This is Jasmine by the way. I'm just calling to say how much I enjoyed spending time with you. And don't worry about that little accident. It's no big deal. So yeah . . . Call me back so we can make plans to see each other again—Oh. One more thing. I told Mitch what you proposed today—we tell each other everything—and he made a good point. Our agreement should be on paper. That's protocol. Legally, I mean. We must have been so caught up in the . . . emotions of the day that we didn't think about it. So call me back and we can do this right.

We're free tonight. Anytime. Okay. Bye, Goldie. Call me back as soon as you can. Bye."

Marigold stood there, her arms aching from holding the wine and Styrofoam container. They hadn't planned for this. They were supposed to be the ones making the calls. They were the predators. She needed to buy time. Come up with a lie. But her head was heavy with memory and empty of ideas.

She made camp in her living room. She'd let Todd keep his room, his besieged stronghold, for one more night. The rest of the house had long been conquered anyway.

She removed the wine's screw cap. A floral perfume emanated from the bottle. Did Riesling need to be aerated? What she needed was its healing properties, not its subtle notes of apricot and not a glass. She swigged from the bottle. She opened the container, squeezed two cubes of ahi tuna between her fingers, and popped them into her mouth. Then the phone rang.

Marigold leaned against the couch and tore open the chopsticks from a disposable paper bag.

Jasmine's voice came through the answering machine. "Marigold, guess what? I stumbled on your address from the birthday cards you sent the boys. You live a lot closer than I thought. I can swing by tonight. What do you say? Sign some papers and give me a quick tour? You know, return the favor from earlier? I'll swing by. You'll be home, right? Where else would you be? You can't drive. Hope you get this. Don't be surprised when you see me at your door."

Marigold turned on the TV and adjusted the brightness to its highest setting. She closed the curtains, locked the doors, and made the whole house dark. Returning to the sole light source, she lowered herself to the floor, bunkered against the couch, and turned off the TV. The chopsticks lost in the darkness, she ate with her hands. The wine bottle soon became slick with sesame oil and soy sauce.

She finished her dinner slowly, letting the juices in her mouth dissolve the fish before swallowing. She was halfway through the Riesling and really had to pee when there was a light knock on the door.

"Goldie," Jasmine said. "Did you get my messages? I need a word." She knocked again. "Maybe she's sleeping."

Marigold plugged one nostril with a finger, hoping to make the sounds of her breathing less detectable.

"Then knock louder." It was a man's voice. He banged on the door. "Marigold. You up?" Mitch shouted. "You have guests."

"Don't be so loud."

"This is our chance. If we want this house, this life, then we have to take it. We deserve more. The kids deserve more. And this is the easy way. Do you want to get pregnant again?"

Together they thumped on the door.

Marigold pulled her knees to her chest to wait out the shelling. The wine would ease her nerves, but burden her bladder, so she refrained.

They twisted the knob. Marigold heard them search the windows for a handle.

"Daddy, when can we go home? I'm sleepy."

"Go back to the car, buddy," Mitch said. "Just a little longer, okay?"

"But I'm really sleepy."

"So sleep. In the car. Like your brother. He's sleeping, right?"

"It's not comfy enough."

"Go draw a picture then. Hey. This big house is going to be ours. There's a pool. Draw us splashing around. Can you do that for me?"

"I don't want to, daddy."

"Freddie, I swear, I'll—"

"We should go," Jasmine said. "She's either not here or she's not opening up."

"Yeah." Mitch kicked the door. "Maybe she died. Let's go."

Marigold waited as long as she could, and when her bladder was about ready to burst, she used the couch to lift herself up. The urge to urinate was so strong she had to hunch over, but she pushed sweet thoughts of relief from her mind and tottered, in the dark, to the phone and made a call.

10

Busboys, stained aprons hanging from their necks, slept walked between tables, refilling water cups and taking orders in Spanish. Solo diners, perched on floor-mounted stools, punctuated each fold of their newspaper with a sigh, blowing out grease-and-coffee-scented air. Their waitress approached, plates balanced on her forearms.

"Excuse me," Eliza said.

The waitress repositioned the condiment caddy. "Whaddya need?"

She stabbed her food with a fork. "My eggs are dry."

"They're over-hard, as per request. You want 'em medium?"

She set down her silverware. "I want them over-hard. But not this dry."

The waitress peered at the grainy yolk. "I'll talk to the chef."

"Please do."

Roger thanked the waitress and assured her of a handsome tip. But she carried on wordlessly, scooting the plate past orders of French toast and club sandwiches sitting in the expo window. She spoke to the sweaty cook, who rolled his eyes and shucked the eggs into the trash.

"So." Marigold peeled open single-serving packets of jam with her teeth. She smeared orange marmalade and grape jelly on triangular pieces of wheat toast. "Nothing on the phone." Her pancakes smothered the life out of a pat of butter. "Nothing in the car." She rearranged her coffee, ice water, and orange juice into a stoplight. "Tell me already."

Roger and Eliza shared a glance and a smile.

"Still waiting."

Roger chopped a log of low sodium sausage. "Got to use the lingo."

"Did you confirm the kill?"

"Six vials. In the recycling bin. With brittle—sorry—we're eating."

"Was that a fist-pump?" Eliza said.

"I'm excited." Marigold reached for her straw. "What did you tell Jasmine to get her to stop bugging me?"

"I said you were staying with me. And I reminded her that the elderly get spooked when they have to move late in life and it's best if the transition is gradual. She believed me once I reminded her that I worked at a rehab hospital."

"That wasn't part of the plan."

"It worked, didn't it? I apologized for you too." Eliza's mouth fell open, and Roger fed her a bite of sausage. Chewing, she said, "I told her Betty couldn't get involved since she's not Todd's lawyer. She took it well. After I explained—for an hour—that the will was legally binding and after giving her Betty's number so she could confirm for herself . . . she took it well." She ate a handful of grapes and spit the seeds into her napkin. "Jasmine's so fake. She said she was worried about you because, apparently, she sensed your desperation to be a mother. And because of this situation, old feelings are back and you can't handle them. So, naturally, you're . . . you're—"

"Unstable."

"More or less."

"What does she think happened to the samples?"

"Blames her boys. Found a screw in their room while vacuuming." Eliza shoveled half of her sister's hash browns onto her plate. "Can't believe you framed the children. You are absolutely heartless."

The bell above the side door chimed. Laughter surged

in. On the patio, college students, donning basketball jerseys and cargo shorts, nursed their hangovers with volcanic Bloody Marys. Their sandals jittered under the table.

When she was their age Marigold went months without wearing socks or sleeves, but now the shade made her shiver. "So what's next?"

"Mr. Popular here"—Eliza poked Roger with the butt of her knife—"got invited to a barbecue next Saturday."

"Where to?"

"Ron's. It's his birthday."

"Ron . . ." Marigold pictured a man with a handlebar mustache. Didn't all Rons have facial hair?

"He's a nobody. His purpose in life is to share obituaries over email and remind people to set their clocks back for daylight saving time."

"Need a plus one?"

"It's a solo job."

"I'm addicted to being out in the field." Marigold missed the pancake and her knife screeched against the plate.

"Hang on."

An adjacent waiter was restocking ceramic containers, filing the sugar and sweetener packets like an accountant during tax season.

"Could you clear this?" Eliza proffered her half-eaten bowl of fruit to him. "Thanks, doll."

The waiter kicked at the swinging doors and disappeared into the kitchen.

"It would be suspicious," Eliza continued, "if you showed up and more samples were destroyed."

"Maybe I'm cursed," Marigold said.

"You are charming when you behave like a child. And it is tempting to humor you. But Roger's got this. Okay?"

Marigold chomped on her toast, which, despite the slather of jam, was dry.

The original waitress reappeared.

Eliza clipped off a sliver of egg. "It's fine."

"More coffee?" the waitress asked.

"I'm good."

"Randall here would be more than happy to—"

"No. Thanks."

"We'll tip in cash," Roger said, but the waitress had turned her attention to the other tables.

"Here's what Roger's going to do." Eliza's fork danced in the air like a conductor's baton. "Bring a few of those mini-kegs to the party—you boys will love that; it will remind you of college—and insist they have to be refrigerated. Inquire about the futuristic freezer and ask if there's room inside for the kegs."

"That's stupid," Roger said. "And I won't be able to unplug it with so many people there."

"You just have to locate it. You'll have the creative liberty to destroy the samples with what you find on site. Like our resident spider." Eliza nudged her sister. "But this is a celebratory brunch. Let's talk strategy at Goldie's."

He smiled. "Don't trust the fine people here?"

In the next booth, rabid children constructed silverware catapults and brewed a potion of malt vinegar and hot sauce. Preteens slapped at the sides of a pinball machine. At the host stand, a group of middle-aged women sifted through a plastic bin of hard candies.

"I don't trust anyone." Eliza said. "Let's go."

"But your food?" Roger said.

"The eggs are dry." She opened her pocketbook. "I'm paying. And don't you tip extra."

11

Marigold opened the door and reflexively glanced at the answering machine. Its red blinking light lured her in like a bug zapper.

"Your phone's preheated," Eliza said.

"One of my gentleman callers," Marigold said. "Leaving me another filthy message."

"Maybe it's Jasmine."

Marigold ushered Roger into the kitchen. "Coffee? Mine's better than the restaurant's."

"There's more bean juice in my veins than blood. You trying to kill me?"

"Tea then?"

Eliza's finger hovered over the machine.

"Lizzie?"

"Settle down. You're the one that's deaf. I hear fine. Not tea. Roger becomes Mr. Bean when he drinks tea."

"It helps digestion."

"Fine."

"It'll be whistling soon."

Eliza thumbed the rotary dial. "You need a new phone."

"New one's upstairs."

"New compared to this relic."

"It was mom's. It reminds me of her."

"Reminds me of being broke." She spun the dial. "It's been so long since I've heard a voicemail. You don't mind?"

"I don't—"

"Hey, Aunt G," Wendy's voice came out in a rush. "Returning your call. I wanted to tell you something, but I guess it will be a surprise. I wish you had a cell phone. So many pictures I want to send you. I'll email you, okay? Print them out and put them on the fridge. You better take down my baby pictures. Okay. Gotta go. Love you. Bye."

The machine offered a list of options. Eliza deleted the message. "What's this surprise?"

"I don't know, Lizzie. It's a surprise." Marigold would excuse herself. Tell them she was more comfortable in her own bathroom for she had eaten a hearty breakfast. She'd open the email and bash out a response if she had time.

"She calls you. She writes you." Eliza knocked over a

card on the mantle. "What do you and my daughter talk about anyway?"

"You're awfully jealous."

"I'm teasing, but can you blame me? She hasn't sent us a Christmas or Easter gift in years. We never receive thank you notes either. I raised her better than that. But people only learn—they can't be taught. You have no idea why she's calling though?"

"I told her I wanted to get her a bathing suit." Marigold made a mental note to check online for swimsuits. "Something Californian. With palm trees and sunset colors."

"One piece or two?"

"Either would do. Wendy has a great figure."

"Please." Eliza headed to the kitchen. "It looks like she stuffs two red onions down her shirt."

"Regardless, they're ripe." She followed her sister. "Why red?"

"Less smell. More crunch."

Chairs were pulled out, ready for butts.

"Thanks, Roger." Marigold took a seat.

Eliza opened to a fresh page in her lavender notebook and wrote out the date. "Goldie, dear. The tea?"

"Right." Marigold filled the kettle, set it on the stove, and turned on the burner. As the water simmered, she located the torn plastic bag—her tea collection. The text on the labels was teeny, so she covertly sniffed the tea bags. She transferred the piles of grassy green and earthy black teas onto a plate and brought them to the table with a carton of soy milk.

"Tea isn't tea without crumpets," Roger said in a clumsy British accent.

"How are you hungry?" Eliza said.

"Not hungry, but a wee peckish."

"I might have cookies," Marigold said.

"Biscuits or blood pudding will do."

Marigold went to the pantry.

"Your eyes that good?" Roger said.

"Better than my ears." Marigold rummaged through the shelves, crinkling bags of tortilla chips and tipping over boxes of cereal. "I have a snack filing system."

"Turn on the light."

"It's busted."

"You got bulbs?"

"In here somewhere."

"I'll change it."

"I got it."

"Can you reach it?"

Eliza jotted something in her notebook. "She's got it."

"I know," Roger said. "I'm not trying to be nice. I'm actually being quite selfish. I can't, bloody cannot have my tea without crumpets."

"Please stop talking like that."

"Faster I drink my tea, the faster you get dull American Roger back."

"Fine. Go. Get away from me."

He entered the pantry, which had the square footage of a fitting room. His breathing strained.

"Claustrophobic?" Marigold said.

"I'm saving the oxygen for you. Got the lightbulb?"

"One second." She turned and checked another shelf.

Her backside brushed against him.

"Oh."

His hot breath went down her neck.

"Sorry," she said. "We're overcapacity."

"Did you find it?"

She found the box and pressed it to his chest. Her eyes had adjusted to the dark and she could see straight up his nostrils.

"It's all about touch." He unscrewed the dead lightbulb. "The last sense to go."

"I'll let you finish up."

"Wait." He wasn't whispering, but he wasn't speaking with his normal volume either. "We have to test it." The new bulb spilled out a few times before he spun it in tight.

"It won't burn the house down?"

"Your home is safe. Turn it on."

They covered their eyes.

"Seven minutes in heaven?" Eliza said when they emerged from the pantry.

"Seven minutes?" Marigold said. "We're faster than a pit crew."

Roger ripped open a package of oatmeal cookies. "We almost called you for help."

"You would like that. But I need your help." She whacked the paper with her pen. "I need intel. Who's going to be at the barbecue and what are they like when they drink?"

The kettle whistled as Roger listed the one-syllable names of the attendees—Ron, Jim, Bill—and their inebriated tendencies. Marigold filled three saucer-less cups. They reviewed contingency plans, prioritized goals, and discussed pick up times and locations. Marigold grunted her agreement to each idea presented to her.

While Eliza made notes, Marigold spied the clock above the stove. It was evening in New York. Wendy had explained how texts and emails were low maintenance plants that required less tending to than calls. But written words were not enough; memorizing her niece's letters hadn't satiated her. She wanted to hear her voice, listen to her blather about her life on the other side of the country. Her niece's stories were slammed full of such minute detail that it took all her concentration to keep them straight in her head. In the process of listening, she forgot about her own life.

"How's that?" Eliza revealed the plan's final blueprint. She circled three stick-limbed men. "Does the spider approve?"

"Looks good. But"—she yawned—"I need a nap."

"We're nearly through."

Marigold took out her hearing aids and rolled them on the table like a pair of dice.

"Fine. Let's talk at home, Rog." Eliza dog-eared the page and mimed: I'll call you.

In a voice that would draw a hush from a librarian, Marigold said, "See yourselves out."

Roger waved.

***

Swaddled in drapes, Marigold peeked out the front window for a third time. The driveway and road were still empty. She grabbed the phone and dialed, each ring sounding hopeful.

But Wendy didn't answer.

In the office, she refreshed the browser. A watched pot never boils, but an email inbox?

If the computer mouse was a real rodent, she would have suffocated it.

Her afternoon plans—chatting with her niece—canceled, she appraised the house. The sitting room was sterile. The chandelier, nestled in the high point of the ceiling, rebuked her for trespassing. She stroked the antique couch's itchy upholstery. Underneath it was a carcass of a robot vacuum, its charging station tossed out weeks ago. Folding her hands, she prayed for earthquakes to rattle the vases of fake flowers to the floor. If earthquakes didn't come, she would rip open the maple hutch and stomp on the crystal glasses like a bride at a Jewish wedding.

She turned on four TVs—all except the flat screen in Todd's room—to the news and pumped the volume. Minuscule lag gave the weatherman a stutter; the forecast was s-s-s-sunny. Crime reports multiplied, echoed. The newscaster's voice followed her, jumbled by the Doppler effect, her house an auditory house of mirrors.

Framed by the windowsill, the pool was a painting, artwork not to be touched.

Unbuttoning her jeans, she patrolled the bathrooms. The cuffs of her pants dragged across the tile as she compared the temperature and welcomeness of each toilet seat.

She walked near, but never into, Todd's room, unsure if the cage's bars would hold.

The TVs screamed of a used car sale. She unlocked and relocked the door. Sober checkpoints were going up in Pacific Beach, the news explained, after a drunk driver survived a crash that killed a graduate student.

In bed, she relived the day with the samples: Jasmine's overwrought face when the vial broke; how gullible she had made her; the heft of the rag. She bottled up that feeling, that thrill. At first, when she opened the bottle, the feeling shot out like shaken-up champagne. But with each opening, the spray grew weaker, flatter.

***

The trash can brimmed with frozen cardboard meal packages. One of Pavlov's dogs, she drooled when the microwave beeped. For hydration, she drank Todd's bourbon. She kept one TV on in the living room, volume at a patter. Cameras panned to late-night hosts and their guests, who threw their heads back in embellished mirth. The jokes didn't reach her though, hearing aids or no.

Did Todd feel like this before he died? As if the hand of a malevolent god had fired up a glue gun and pasted him to his chair.

When she managed to shut the TV off, she lay supine for hours, playing in her lucid daydreams. She imagined the barbecue. The middle-aged grill master blackening burgers, kids slaloming between their parents' legs, and the striped polo shirt Roger wore to outdoor occasions. She squeezed her eyes shut until they hurt and mustered up Roger's speech—the ruse he'd use to steal a gander at the samples. Often, she infiltrated the scene to scrap Roger's plan and go rogue, firing vials like poison darts.

But when she played through all her imagination's iterations, she had to wake up and confirm the kill. She faced the phone and gave it loving attention.

Silence.

She feigned apathy, hoping it would make the first move. But the phone ignored her. Ignored her even as she put her ear to it to check its dial tone, to check its pulse.

The glue hardened. She was a figurine; the house, a diorama. The front door drifted away like a string-less balloon. On the floor were capless Sharpies and yellow snowballs of balled-up legal pad paper—letters addressed to Wendy. They listed the clothes and jewelry and books she wanted her to have. She didn't recognize her handwriting; it was a ransom letter's scrawl, random letters capitalized, random words in cursive. The marker had bled through the paper and stained the coffee table black.

She slept on the couch. She wasn't tired, but slumber exploded from the two nightly sleeping pills she washed down with sink water and spit.

12

The soap opera villain was belligerently phoning his ex. Marigold flung her arms and kicked her legs like a tipped-over turtle. Entrenched on the couch, she searched for the remote. Her hands ducked under the cushions, while her bare feet scoured the coffee table. She opened her eyes and found the remote, but the TV was already off.

Wendy.

She stood. Woozy, she hugged the armchair. When enough blood cells swam to her brain, she answered the phone. "Wendy?"

"Hello, over," Roger said. "Mayday. Mayday. Hello, over."

"Hey."

"Hello, over."

"How'd it go?"

"I said, 'hello, over.'"

She sighed. "Roger that, Roger. So how'd it go?"

"It's Monday."

"I got you—my calendar. How could I forget? But the

barbecue. How'd it go?"

"We can talk about that later. You have to eat. Grow big and strong. And food doesn't grow on trees, you know."

"I have plenty of microwavable—"

"Can't hear you. Vroom. Vroom. Already getting in my car."

She chuckled. "Fine. I have to get ready though. Let yourself in."

She unlocked the door and hurried up the stairs. Stepping into the shower, she was unsure of her body. Like a lethargic bear gearing up after hibernation. She strangled the bottle for the last drops of shampoo. While rinsing out the conditioner, she sang a few notes of "Yellow Submarine," a song played to death on Roger's favorite radio station.

She buttoned a cardigan and dried her ears before putting in her hearing aids.

Roger arrived. He closed the door with gentleness.

"I'll be right down," she called to him.

"I'll be outside."

***

Marigold exited the house and locked the door. "How'd it go at Ron's?"

"Hold on." Roger stood on one foot. His arms flapped for balance.

"What are you doing?"

"Ankle stability." He switched feet. "Had a scare this morning. I don't want to rile you up." Bipedalled, he opened the passenger door. "But I was in the shower." He swung to his side and hopped in. "It was wet and—"

"This is inappropriate."

"I nearly fell."

"Get a non-slip mat. Let's pick one up today."

"We have one," Roger said as they pulled onto the road. "But the gap between what my brain says and what my body does is expanding like the universe."

"Not you too. You never complain about your body."

"I am confident in it."

"I'm serious. 'My neck hurts. My back aches. I'm going in for a procedure next week. Had a scare this morning.'" She dropped her granny impersonation. "It's all you hear from people our age."

"What else do we have to talk about?"

"There's silence." Warm air seeped in through the cracked windows. "Unless you want to tell me about the barbecue?"

"Silence then," he said and turned on the radio.

They listened to songs of lost money, lost love, and the morning rain. Familiar road signs flew by. In surrounding vehicles, adults yapped away on headsets, while their babies, strapped in car seats, chewed on teething rings.

They missed their usual exit.

"Are you kidnapping me?" Marigold said. "I shouldn't have showered. Did nothing but tempt you."

"It's strategic." He checked the rearview mirror. "In case we're being followed." The car accelerated, matching the speed of his speech. "I hadn't drank that much since our wedding."

"Roger."

They zoomed through a yellow light. The engine grunted from overexertion. "Remember? We ran out of wine and all we had was tequila? Even my grandparents were licking salt and sucking limes."

She gripped his forearm. "You're scaring me."

"Sorry." He tapped the brakes. "I'm only thinking of myself. If we fly off the road, they'll hook me up to you and give me all your blood." They got over to the slow lane. "Not everyone has that luxury." He glanced at her. "But you remember?"

She exhaled and let go of his arm. "I took the picture of you behind the bar."

"I love that photo."

"You were so handsome."

"So were you."

"Thanks?"

"You wore red."

"You remember that?"

"Of course."

"You weren't too drunk?"

"It was a memorable night."

"Yeah. Until—"

"The guy was swamped." He regripped the wheel. "We

should have hired another bartender. It was our fault."

"The tip was generous."

"We were in the foxhole together. I had to reward him."

"You're right."

They stopped at a red light, the car panting. He stroked the dashboard.

"Tell me what happened," she said. "Confirm the kill."

"Eliza's rough draft needed refinement." He blew on his fingernails.

"Still waiting."

"So here's what I did." He turned down a wide street, toward the supermarket.

"Yes?"

"I got them all fucking drunk."

Marigold howled with laughter.

"I usurped total control. I had them take shots for everything. If they were wearing sunglasses. If they had ever colored their hair. A shot for each pork rib they had polished off."

"They followed your orders?"

"They didn't need much push. Anyway, we—"

"One question. Were you wearing a polo?"

"I don't remember. Why?"

"I want to picture all the details."

"Picture this. Jim and his ponytail doing a mini keg stand. We attracted a crowd with that stunt. Little kids piled out of the bounce house and teenagers put down their phones to count how long we could drink." Beyond the bug-splattered windshield, an older man, hauling bags of aluminum cans, straddled the space between two lanes of cars. Roger slowed down and shielded the jaywalker until he reached the sidewalk. "When the keg was tapped, there was this . . . expectation. We had to perform. So I brought up party tricks. I did my go-to."

"With the matches?"

"That one's a crowd-pleaser, but it's not my go-to. You think that's my best?"

"Is this a test?"

"Come on, you love it. You know."

"You do a lot of tricks."

"You know . . . Eliza says it's a waste, but it's still edible."

"The apple trick?"

"Granny Smith, Fiji, McIntosh. They all crumble in my grasp."

"So you ripped apart the vials?"

Roger put a knee to the steering wheel and flaunted his hands as if he were a pianist. "No blood, gunk, or glass here."

They parked and sat still, seat belts fastened across their chests like sashes. Customers slogged to their cars, plastic bags coiled around their wrists. Children lounged in shopping carts, heads resting on packs of toilet paper, loaves of bread in their laps. A father tore open an ice pop with his teeth and gave it to his son.

"Bill juggled," Roger said. "Avocados. Beer bottles. I took side bets on whether he could juggle certain items. Losers had to drink. Bill drank regardless. He did hot dogs. Grilling utensils, tongs and spatulas. But I pushed him to do more. And the crowd . . . I was like their mother bird. They were eating out of my mouth."

"That's not the expression."

"So I went for it. And I . . . I said . . ."

"You want me to beg for it?"

"I said: Would you stake a life on your juggling?"

She smacked his thigh. "I need new ears after hearing that garbage."

"Out came the samples. Bill squeezed on these purple gloves." Roger unbuckled his seatbelt. "We were seeing double, triple. And I challenged him to juggle in the driveway, over cement. I put my money on gravity. He got up to four vials, but he couldn't do all six."

"Well done." She rubbed the spot where she had hit him. "So you've bought in? You're ready for the next phase of the plan?"

"Can't stay on first base our whole lives, even if it's safe." The automatic doors parted. He chose a cart from the corral and shoved it forward and yanked it backward. When he was satisfied the wheels were aligned and lubricated, he said, "We have to make a play for second, even if we get thrown out."

"I only know what second base meant in high school."

Roger coughed. "Where should we start? We have no list, no map. The world is ours."

***

Anesthetized by the supermarket's jingle, they meandered through the aisles, perusing each shelf, seasonal display, and freezer like museum exhibits. Roger fondled a pair of oranges, pressed them to his chest, and shimmied. She lent him her glasses as they conferred over a can of cannellini beans, ammo for his chili recipe.

"You want pork chops?" Roger said, examining the Styrofoam-packaged meat.

Marigold leaned on the shopping cart. "I hate pork chops."

"You make them all the time."

"I did."

"For Todd?"

"He hated them too. But he loved the horseradish sauce he slathered on them."

"Now you can get whatever you want."

Tortillas, chocolate milk, Greek yogurt, cans of peaches and prunes, and a jar of green olives—for the vodka—occupied the cart. She memorized the prices, but the numbers swimming in her head wriggled free as she calculated. Her allowance card hadn't been filled in months.

Elderly folks buzzed around on souped-up shopping carts. Roger volunteered to grab their calcium tablets and laundry detergent from the top shelves.

Groceries advanced down the conveyor belt. The total popped up. Discounts and her rewards membership sliced the price.

"I got this." Roger extended his credit card.

She hit his arm with a grocery divider. "Somebody stop this man." She fished out her wallet, dropped it. To the cashier, she flashed her fakest smile. "Don't take that—I'm warning you. This is the one you want."

The cashier stared at the pieces of plastic thrusted at her. She tucked her bangs into her visor. "This usually happens at restaurants." Behind them, a line of shoppers doglegged to the left. "And it's charming. But this isn't a restaurant."

"Men." Marigold crammed the card into her wallet. "Always have to provide."

***

Back at the car, Marigold jerked the seat belt strap like a ripcord.

"I wanted to treat you," he said, barely audible over the hum of the engine.

"Bull shit. Manure—as your wife would say."

"I thought that . . ." They reached the parking lot's exit and waited to merge.

"Are you incapable of multitasking? Talk and drive."

"It's—"

"I can afford groceries."

"Can you?"

She didn't know. "I'll pay you back. If the plan works."

"It'll work."

"What's the next part of the plan anyway? We should know."

"We have to trust Eliza."

"I've done that my whole life."

"Allan's the next target. She's close with his wife. For now, that's the only way to get to him. So—"

"I know." Marigold counted her breaths. Palm trees and a strip mall rolled by. The headrest cradled her skull.

Her eyes closed, she relaxed her body and swayed with each turn until they pulled into her driveway.

"Marigold?"

"You don't need to say my name. I'm right here." She opened her eyes and smiled. "Roger."

"Can I ask you a question?"

"You don't need permission."

"Have you talked to Wendy?"

"We're playing phone tag."

"I've been calling and texting her too." He popped the trunk and carried the bags inside.

Marigold slid a chair in front of the fridge. Sitting, she threw out the expired bottles of ranch and hot sauce—though they claimed squatter's rights—and stocked the fresh groceries.

With seizure-inducing speed, Roger tested and retested the pantry lightbulb.

"She donates blood. She volunteers, " he said, continuing their conversation as if a bookmark had kept its place. He rolled the eco-bags and stuffed them in a drawer. "But the cement around her soul hasn't hardened yet."

"Don't worry." Marigold pushed the chair back to the table. "She's like her father."

"That may not be a good thing." He had something behind his back. "Close your eyes and put your hands out."

"This feels fun." She set the fifth of vodka on the counter. "Shots?"

"I'm much too refined for shots." He cracked open the bottle. "Where are your fancy glasses?"

It took some time to track down the shaker, vermouth, and extra-long bar spoon. While he stirred the martinis, Marigold skewered olives with toothpicks.

Roger sampled his cocktail. "How about after this," he said, coughing. "We go out?"

Marigold bit into a vodka-soaked olive. "But it's a school night."

"There's that place down the street. We have to climb a few stairs to get in, but we can walk to it. We won't have to cook and they might check our IDs at the door. We—"

"Let's go."

"But I have more reasons."

"Quick." Marigold drained the rest of her drink. "Before the spontaneity wears off."

13

The bar booths were red and white. License plates covered the walls. Through closed captions, announcers lauded athletes running around the diamond and sparring in the ring. Bartenders slammed napkins on the bar top as if trying to squish an elusive bug. White-collar colleagues drank their first round in silence. Refueled, they gossiped about their boss, leaning close, blouses grazing against shirt sleeves. From the dining area came the singing and clapping of the birthday song.

The waiter cleared a ravaged plate of chicken wings. "Another round for the happy couple?"

"Actually—"

"He has to call his wife first," Marigold said.

The waiter and Roger both turned red. The latter took out his phone and peeped the time. "It's early. And she—"

"We're brother and sister," Marigold said and the waiter's customer service smile returned.

"She's the funny one," Roger said.

Loyal to her spirit, Marigold stuck with vodka, while he explored the happy hour cocktail menu.

Couldn't they pretend for one night? She didn't need a soulmate. She didn't need him, just someone to binge greasy food and have one too many with. They could sleep together. And stay in bed until the next afternoon. Not hungover. Okay, maybe a little. Crusted eyelids opening one at a time. Feet sticking out from the covers. Touching. Being touched. Laughing at stupid jokes and sharing dreams and plans for the future. Plans like the words she's read and the words she knows the meanings of, but words she's never spoken. But when she tells him her plans he doesn't laugh when she mispronounces them though she sounds silly. Because he knows these plans are anything but silly. They're sacred. Forged in the fires of the soul.

Roger settled for another beer and ordered nachos.

"Is she plotting tonight?"

He nodded. "She's obsessed."

"We all are."

"To a degree," he said. "Anger is an effective fuel, but it doesn't burn clean."

His frothy-headed beer arrived. The table's ringworm, a rash of condensation, spread.

"But she is doing this for you."

"Is she?" She squeezed a lime into her vodka soda. "She hates Todd."

"She loves you more than she hates him. She took care of him for you. And she knows how hard you've had it."

"I never wanted kids," she said, perhaps too quickly.

"Still. She's trying to help. Not that she has much choice. It's like . . ." Roger bulldozed a tortilla chip through a mound of salsa, guacamole, and sour cream. "We're sifting sand. My pan has wide holes. I catch the big stuff—rocks and shells—while the sand passes through. But Eliza's pan has no holes. She holds onto everything. Everything."

"You and your analogies. So is that why she's so . . ."

He laughed. "People are assholes to their family."

"Then Eliza's kin to all."

Roger lifted his glass. "Sun." He pointed to a jalapeño slice. "Moon." He scanned the table, his eyes coming to rest on his left hand. Hesitating a moment, he tugged at his wedding band. "Earth."

"Is this how you teach your classes?"

He positioned the three round objects in a straight line. "Her good days come as often as a solar eclipse. Celestial fucking bodies have to align for her to be her lovely self. But when they align, it's beautiful. Even if it lasts a moment."

"I've never seen an eclipse."

"Never?"

"Not even a partial."

"Marigold." Her name sounded different when he said it. Like the acoustic version of a familiar song. "You've seen one. As a kid at least."

"I'd remember something so beautiful."

"Maybe you didn't know what you were seeing. Be right back." He slipped his ring back on and asked the bartender where the restroom was.

She scooped up a chunk of congealed cheese and recalled the positive memories of her sister. Eliza, though cold, was annoyingly reliable. She spoke to Todd after Marigold described the mass that came out of her, the mass she had to dispose of with kitchen gloves. All four times, she spoke to him so Marigold didn't have to. For better or worse, Eliza convinced Todd to bypass a postnuptial when he received his inheritance. And of course, she gave birth to Wendy.

"Men are filthy." Roger burped into his hand. "So much piss on the floor, I had to stand like a giraffe drinking water."

She smiled at him. His anger was the anger of children. Too cute to take seriously.

Patches of young people had sprouted like dandelions. They pounded tabletops for hits and knocked back tequila shots for runs. On the bar were crumpled singles next to empty pint glasses.

"How are you sleeping?" Roger said.

"Why? Tired?"

"I can't sleep well these days."

"Hope it's not guilt."

"I don't know. What about you?"

"I sleep fine."

"You do?"

The alcohol urged her on. "I have nightmares though."

"Recurring?"

"Not every night, but often. I'm in the house. Todd's apnea is bad, so I go to check on him, but he's not in his room. So I follow the snores and snorts and the choking. There's a lot of choking.

"But I can't find him, and the choking is getting worse, so I panic. I'm moving so fast I'm flying, but the house is a maze and not mine, so I stop and get my bearings. But now Todd is screaming. And it's coming from the walls. So I tear at them—the walls—and I rip the plaster and stucco— whatever it's called—but there's nothing there and it's quiet. For a moment. And then there are more . . . sounds. In another part of the house, behind another wall." She stabbed the lime with her straw.

"You never reach him? That's how it ends?"

She wasn't going to tell him how it ends, how she stuffs a sock in his mouth and plugs his nostrils shut—she wasn't that drunk. She slurped up the dregs of her drink. "Why can't you sleep?" Her hand was on the table, palm up, there if he needed it. "Nightmares too?"

A smile glittered across his face. "I have this recurring dream that any toilet I use overflows and floods the bathroom with . . . discharge."

"Oh." Her hand retreated to her lap.

"I'm talking nonsense. Shall I walk you home?"

"Finish your drink first."

"I had too much. It's not my wedding night."

Roger paid, and they walked down the stairs hugging the handrail.

"Are you cold?" he said.

She linked her arm with his. "I haven't been out in so long." In the clear sky, the moon was curved into a sly smile.

Stopped at a crosswalk, they quizzed each other on the constellations. The bright dots clustered together like braille, symbols they couldn't understand.

"This reminds me of the night at Lake Arrowhead." He slowed their pace as they approached the house. "We thought Todd died."

"You wanted to call an ambulance." She slipped the key into the lock. "But Eliza nursed him through. Made him puke it all up."

"We couldn't sleep. Remember?"

She led him inside. "I still have splinters from that chair swing."

Sinuous shadows contorted and climbed the walls. But they were her shadows in her house and she wasn't scared.

"Do you remember the sunrise?" Roger asked.

The sun had been at its weakest, rising blearily over

the horizon. They stared at it while they could like it was a sleeping lion beginning to stir.

Marigold set the dimmer switch low. "Did you want to call Lizzie?"

"In a bit." He plunked down on the couch and groaned. "I'm old."

"Don't say that," she said. "Need water? Medicine?"

"What about fire?" He kicked at the fireplace. "Does it work?"

She dug around for the remote. Fake flames danced over fake logs.

Roger slid to the floor and stretched out in front of the fireplace. His joints popped like frying bacon.

"I'll get you a pillow."

"Don't go," he said. "Come here."

"Roger."

"Come here."

Marigold sank to the floor and leaned against the armchair. "You drunk?"

"The room always spins, right?" He laughed. "I'm fine.

I'm a waterbed, but I'm fine. Do me a favor?"

"You want that pillow?"

He jiggled his stomach. His shirt lifted slightly to reveal his belly hair. "Does this feel okay to you?"

"I'm not a doctor."

"And I won't sue for malpractice."

She gazed at the swirly patch of gray grass, a field of play, poking out from his shirt. Her fingertip slipped into his navel. "It's bubbling."

"Tell me what it sounds like."

She looked at his face, tinted orange in the firelight. "I'll crush you."

"I'll survive."

She lowered herself and pressed her ear to his warm belly. His shirt tickled.

"What do you hear?" he asked.

"There's a creature swimming inside you."

"Follow it."

She sailed over the waves of his breath, rolling up and

down, up and down. The creature swam and fed and digested. She touched his calf. Air puffed from his lips. His knee was hard and mostly round, like a baby's skull. His thigh was surprisingly tight. She prodded for his hip bone, found it, and followed it inwards.

"Marigold."

"Hmm?"

"I should call Eliza."

14

Fog and darkness mingled at dawn. They hugged goodbye. She looked up at him. She wanted him to see her, wanted their eyes to meet. But his gaze was fixed on the door. Nuzzled against his chest, she inhaled the scent of her lemongrass body wash on him. His stubble prickled her forehead. Standing there in the foyer, she gripped him like the lid of a tight jar that refused to budge.

***

No hangover symptoms but she felt shitty. She swished cold coffee like mouthwash. On the couch armrest doing the splits was a book, What Happens at Night by Peter Cameron.

She drove her fingers into her scalp, reaching for the shriveled frontal lobe and dilapidated memory stores. She wanted to punish her brain for its decisions and the unprompted flashbacks starring Todd and Roger.

To distract her mind, she gave it simple tasks. Like a substitute teacher assigning busywork. She sorted the recycling, relined the garbage cans, and watered the succulents in her bay window with an eyedropper. She tore off the bedding and ran the washing machine. The pillows, stripped, feathers poking out, waited for a costume change.

Outside, the sun had incinerated the fog. She removed the pool cover and made an appointment for a cleaning that afternoon.

Eat and bathe.

But her stomach was a raisin. She called Wendy and left a placid message when she didn't pick up.

She showered, moisturized, and tumbled into bed, arms folded across her chest like a mummified pharaoh. The curtains floated on a steady breeze. From the ceiling, the fan spun listlessly. To keep the flashbacks at bay, she employed a Todd-tested sleeping technique and counted by three.

Three, six, nine.

Would the nightmares haunt her naps too?

Three, six, nine, twelve, fifteen.

What did the mirror see last night?

Three, six, nine, twelve, fifteen, eighteen, twenty-one, twenty-four.

Heat tingled beneath her skin.

Did someone open an oven?

She flipped and reflipped her pillow, but both sides

were balmy. Kicking free of the duvet, she charged the window. But the breeze was flaccid, pitiful, a sailor's scorn. She rushed to the bathroom, hair clinging to her neck, and doused water on her wrists and armpits.

But sweat continued to drip.

Would panting work? She tore off her clothes and jerked the nozzle to the blue C. She clamored into the shower as if snagging the last seat on a lifeboat. Frozen rain pelted her. Air caught in her chest. Her arms flailed. Water skimmed over her face, her mouth opening and closing in gulps like a feeding whale. She got out, shivering but hot, clothes scattered about like a disorganized fitting room.

She limped to bed, wet and naked. On the sheet her body's outline was traced in moisture. She took a couple deep breaths and composed herself.

From the top:

Three, six, nine.

The phone rang.

She whaled on the pillow, punching, choking, and chewing on its corners.

"I bet you're hungry."

"Lizzie," Marigold said. "I'm napping."

"You a baby? Let's get lunch."

"Can't. The pool guy's coming."

"Craving a different sort of meat, eh? Last night whet your appetite?"

"I'll call you later."

"When will the pool boy be finished with you? I have to tell you something."

15

The pool guy sprayed chemicals and inspected the filter for leaves and rodents. When he finished, Marigold wrangled him in with small talk and a refreshing beverage. She didn't want to be alone. She acted enthralled as he listed the strangest things he had found in a pool—used condoms, a baby skunk, still alive. After his third glass of iced tea, he said he had to get going. She walked him out and manned the gates for her sister's arrival.

On a shelf by the door was a bowl filled with coins and keys emblazoned with a jungle cat, a galloping horse, and a three-pointed star. Marigold dipped her hand into the metal soup of loose change. To keep the feeling of dread from swallowing her, she counted the coins. Then she solved simple equations, subtracting six pennies from four dimes and a nickel.

She could handle this. Make eye contact. Don't stutter. Joke, but don't overdo it.

The RAV4 pulled into the driveway, heaving.

Marigold opened the door.

Eliza breezed in wearing a burgundy blouse. "Dining table."

"Hi, Roger."

He shook his head slightly and proceeded to the dining room.

Was it a warning?

"You coming?" Eliza said. "We can talk in the bedroom if that's where you're more comfortable."

Marigold set a stack of quarters on the shelf.

"Tongue too tired from last night?"

"I haven't seen you," Marigold said. "Haven't—"

"Oh you talk fine."

"—heard from you. I don't know what's going on."

"Let's get back on the same page. Come on."

"I recited lines." Marigold continued to the living room and dropped in the recliner. She sat like Lincoln in his memorial. "I practiced character voices. We wrote and rehearsed scripts. For Roger, we organized a schedule to the minute. We had process goals, outcome goals, performance goals. And I don't know anything about Allan. He's the biggest threat. We should all be involved."

"Calm down." She went to the next room and beckoned Roger.

He stood in the doorway with a funeral face. Eliza made a sound with her mouth and he found a spot on the couch.

"Goldie's holding court in here." Eliza sauntered to the fireplace and tapped the glass. "You're right, Rog, this is homey." She sat next to him and put her head on his shoulder. "You should turn it on for me sometime. Or is it only for special occasions?"

"I use it when I'm cold," Marigold said. "Are you cold?"

"I'm still hot from yesterday." Eliza jittered like a cooped-up dog about to be walked. "So I arrived after dinner, my famous—now infamous—blondie bars in tow. Added an extra ingredient." She drummed her fingers on the coffee table. "Fast-acting laxatives."

"Allan ate them?"

"He was out bowling. Have you been to his house?"

"No."

"Hideous. Red vinyl furniture, linoleum flooring, and one bathroom. One. Carol kept her dignity. Unfortunately. But her sons—Allan's boys—had to fight over the kitchen sink."

"Carol's your friend."

"It's war and she's on the wrong side of the border." Her voice quickened. "It was glorious. The scene unfolded in slow motion. Carol was screaming from the toilet. The boys had their pants around their ankles, stumbling like they were running a three-legged race. They left brown trails. One squatted on the balcony and had to use a plastic bag to—

"Wait," Marigold said.

"Don't interrupt."

"Did Roger hear this already?"

"He bought the laxatives," Eliza said.

"This was yesterday. And you didn't tell me?"

Roger crossed his arms.

"Relax," Eliza said. "He doesn't know the rest. While they . . . defecated, I searched for the Cryo Magic 2000."

"Did you contaminate it with fecal matter?" Marigold said.

"I checked the rooms, under the beds. Stupid. Allan came home toting his ball bag—I called it a ball sack. I offered him a blondie, but it reeked so bad by then he had no appetite."

"Did you talk?"

"We chatted outside."

"What he say? Where was the freezer?"

"He told me . . . He told me I missed an opportunity."

"To do what? Those days are behind you."

"Not me. He said we should have inseminated Wendy."

"Mother fucker," Roger said. "I'll send him to his brother."

Eliza massaged his ear, but he shook free and stormed out the room.

"Allan's an asshole," Marigold said. "It's not news. He's acting like Allan suggested incest."

She waved her hand in dismissal. "Allan showed me the document from the fertility clinic. His step-daughter's pregnant."

Marigold flinched. "Already?" A trap door in her stomach fell open. Air rushed in.

"Allan convinced his family to pool their samples," Eliza said. "Got them reanalyzed and selected the best specimens. He promised to sell everything, save a car or two, and split the money."

"So should I pack my stuff?"

"I have a plan, but it's blurry." She smacked her lips. "Got any liquid inspiration from last night?"

"There's vodka."

"You get the booze and I'll get Roger. I'll give him the update."

The freezer's breath hung in the air. Tubs of sorbet stood sentry. Marigold pushed them aside and located the vodka, stamping her fingerprints on the frosty bottle. She put it on the table with a glass and a jug of grapefruit juice.

She watched Eliza and Roger pace around the pool. From time to time, Roger would stick his toe in the water. Eliza had to grab the back of his shirt to keep him from falling in. She brought him off the pool ledge, and they hugged. They did a few more laps around the pool and then stopped in a place where the light didn't reach.

Marigold's heart struggled to beat. As if it was torn from her chest and submerged in sand. But her whole body was buried in sand. The sand from her life's hourglass. It came up to her mouth and filled her ears. The trickle of sediment falling from above was weak. She only had a few good years left. And they were going to be hers. If she couldn't own them or control them—then she didn't want them. But it wouldn't come to that. She'd escape one way or another. She'd order more sleeping pills.

The couple came in hand in hand.

"This won't do," Eliza said. "My liver has an itch, and I can't scratch it alone." She grabbed two more glasses and shoved them under the ice dispenser. In the avalanche, stray cubes fell to the floor, which she kicked under the fridge.

"I don't want to," Roger said.

"Quell your anger." She ran the faucet and appraised her vodka water. Grimacing, she said, "Drink with me. I'm your wife." She pushed a glass in front of him.

"Pass the juice."

Marigold shook the jug and poured. Pulpy juice splashed over the rim and onto the table. "You want some?"

"I'm not drinking for pleasure." Eliza took another sip and scrunched up her face. "Inspiration comes from pain. Cheers."

Their glasses came together shyly.

"Now no plan B is ideal, so keep an open mind." Eliza swirled her drink. "We have to induce a miscarriage."

"Really?" Roger said.

"That word isn't going to make her self-destruct."

Marigold drank deeply and said, "Despite my experience, I'm no expert." Her tongue flicked over her teeth like windshield wipers. "But we can shove her down some stairs."

"That's an idea."

"Or use a coat hanger."

"To churn her insides."

"You're not funny," Roger said.

"Nothing's changed but the location," Eliza said. "We destroyed samples before. Now we'll destroy them inside a body.

"Remember," Marigold said. "We can't stay on first base our whole lives."

16

"Swing by the store for me," Eliza said. "And think about it."

Roger took out his key ring and spun it around his finger. "What do you want?"

"Booze."

"Anything specific?"

She downed the rest of her vodka. "You know what I like."

As he was heading out, he stopped and said to Marigold, "Do you want anything?"

"You know what she likes too," Eliza said. He left, and she adopted his abandoned Greyhound. "Sisters."

"Sisters," Marigold repeated like a bored student in a foreign language class. Their glasses clinked. "You hungry?" She went to the fridge. "I got food."

"I don't want to cook."

"The microwave does all the work."

"Sit. You're making me anxious. Making me drink more." Eliza cleared half the glass in one go. "You think he'll get beer?"

"You didn't tell him to."

"Beer's my favorite. But I like wine too. What's your favorite?"

"Vodka."

"You think he'll get your vodka?"

"I didn't ask for it so . . . I'm hungry. Let's order pizza."

"I'll call."

"I'll do it. I got the number in the other room."

They agreed on an order, and Marigold crept to the living room. She opened drawers, wrong drawers, empty drawers. When she found the phone number stamped on a magnet, she dropped it under a cabinet.

She opened the curtains. It was twilight and the neighbors had their porch lights on. Driveways were full: parents home from work; teenagers home from school. Across the street a father and daughter played wiffle ball on their front lawn. When he struck her out a second time, he reminded her to keep her eye on the ball.

Will the neighbors notice when she's gone? Only if she leaves in a coroner's van. Are they going to welcome Allan into their community, the one Marigold had only observed? It made sense. He had kids. But he was so . . . slimy. And she was . . .

"I don't hear you ordering," Eliza shouted.

Marigold descended to her knees like the tin man, unlocking one joint at a time, and picked up the magnet.

"I'm well, thank you," she said into the phone. "And yourself? Glad to hear. My order. Hmm. I'll have two pizzas. One large. One medium. On the large pie—pie? Who am I?" She laughed. "I'm from here. And you? Do I detect an accent?"

Her sister strode in and double-tapped her invisible wristwatch.

"I'll have a large pepperoni and a medium veggie." Marigold gave the address and hung up.

"Let's chat in here." Eliza laid on the couch, clutching her glass. "Pass me the quilt."

Marigold tucked her sister in.

"It's been you and me for a long time," Eliza said. "I feel like I know you. But I only see what you show me. Isn't that right?"

"No, you've seen all of me, Lizzie."

"You're a small pool."

"And you're drunk." If she was lucky the pizza guy would overshoot the driveway and smash through the front window.

"People assume you're shallow because they can't see to the bottom."

"I don't know if I should cut you off or get you another."

"I'll wait for the reinforcements." She tilted the glass over her face. Drops of vodka water splashed her cheeks.

Marigold took the glass from her. "I'll grab you a towel."

"Do you have restless leg syndrome?" Eliza wiped her face with the quilt. "Sit."

"Yes, master." Marigold climbed into the recliner.

"I didn't tell Roger, but Allan said something funny."

"About the blondies?"

"About you. He says you killed Todd."

Marigold snorted. "Okay."

"You cooked his meals. Could have slipped something in."

"I should have. Before he changed the will."

"We'd understand." Eliza considered her like she was an item up for auction.

"What are you looking at?"

She sucked in a breath. "Forget Allan. Greedy people like him assume rich people like you are all evil."

"I'm not rich and I'm not evil."

"You are a survivor. I thought you'd end up like mom."

"That doesn't mean the same thing to me as it does to you."

"You have her ears. And you were both pretty things, but mom was—"

"Do we have to talk about this?"

"After dad died, when we were broke—"

"She made it work." They had white bread and peanut butter and enough clothes between them for a week's worth of outfits. During the summer, they survived their AC-less apartment by sleeping with frozen water bottles tucked under their necks and between their thighs. And in the mornings, they drank the melted water for breakfast.

"I don't care about her chastity. I'm talking about her job. I don't blame her. I respect her. I blame dad. Going off and dying and leaving us nothing. But after, we had to distract ourselves. Distract ourselves from the hurt. Mom worked—though she didn't last too long. I went to church and you . . ." Eliza pondered for a bit. "You stopped talking."

"I talk," Marigold said. "When I have something to say."

"That's bad. Being in your head all the time. One day you're going to explode."

Marigold hid her smile. If she had a fuse, it was an infinite tail, its end burning a lifetime away.

"But until then," Eliza said, "you need this inheritance. I told you. The plan came to me in a dream. I visited Todd in the hospital. I was dressed in a nurse's uniform, but instead of the cross, the emblem on my cap was a sperm, floating down the fallopian tube.

"The paged me on the intercom, and I knew exactly what to do. I scrubbed my hands and entered the operating room. There was a blue surgical towel covered with clamps, retractors, 10 blades, and other tools I don't know the names of. I chose a syringe, the barrel as thick as my wrist, and plunged it into his hairy, wrinkly walnut balls. I wanted the needle to come out the other side.

"I connected a tube and emptied his semen into a bucket. When the tube got clogged, I jiggled it and jolted his balls. He screamed." She paused, listened. A wind chime played softly. "When the procedure was done, I dumped the bucket into a dumpster."

"A vasectomy would have been easier."

"Tell my subconscious. Remember my rehab clinic?"

Marigold had volunteered there. She announced bingo numbers and hosted trivia, quizzing the residents on the state capitals.

"I still smell it," Eliza said. "And no matter how much lotion I use, my hands are always dry. Dry from giving bed baths. Took me for—ev—er—to—speak—nor—ma—ly. Wendy hated when I talked to her like a patient. I felt sorry for them though. No one chooses to have a stroke."

"Did you feel sorry for Todd?"

"I hated him for how he treated you."

"But you quit your job to take care of him."

"That was a coincidence."

"You did take care of him."

"You couldn't. Or wouldn't."

"I hired nurses. So why?"

Eliza craned her neck to the headlights shining through the window. "It was the Christian thing to do."

***

Roger unpacked whiskey, tonic water, a case of German beer, wine, and a jug of grapefruit juice.

The pizza arrived. Eliza paid, and they set up shop in the dining room.

Roger poured the wine. Drops trickled down the bottle, blazing crooked red trails over the label.

Eliza ripped off the top of the pizza box and tore the cardboard into square plates. "No dishes," she said, flinging the squares like frisbees.

Marigold folded a slice and shoved it in her mouth. The pizza was salty and hot and delicious. She felt her blood coagulate but chewed out the worry.

Slices continued to settle in her stomach like neatly

aligned Tetris blocks. Parmesan snowflakes dotted the table. Glasses of wine—for the sisters, at least—became mugs of beer. Marigold laughed at Eliza's thorny jokes and offered Roger the slices with the heaviest toppings. "This is going down too easy," she said.

Alcohol had always been fun for her. In college, she and her roommates held a weekend pre-party ritual. On blessed nights, they excavated enough coins from their purses to splurge on sodas. Most nights though, bunched around the sticky kitchen counter—their altar—they chased shots with milk and cigarettes. Between toasts and outfit changes, they chattered like kids waiting to ride a roller coaster, predicting who would scream the loudest and guessing who might throw up.

Funneling the rest of the liquor into water bottles, they traversed the campus. The walk to the party was the bridge between expectations and reality. But the party wasn't real either.

The border walls separating her senses fell. Music shook her bones. Vodka—poured from the bottle straight into her mouth—scorched her taste buds. Desperate rock climbers searched her body for handholds; fingers slipped between belt loops.

Like hermit crabs ditching their shells, tongues crawled

free and searched for new homes.

The first time a tongue was lodged in her mouth, she wrestled it into submission. But the second time, she danced with it. She soon learned no two people had the same rhythm.

Back at their apartment, they microwaved cheese quesadillas and slurped bowls of cereal. Marigold chugged Gatorade and Tylenol and slept naked with her makeup on. Lusty hot rod engines sang her to sleep. Images from the night flashed across her eyelids. Images that memory couldn't capture. So the next weekend, they were back in line to experience the roller coaster ride again.

"Wait till you stand," Eliza said.

"Who needs to wait?" Marigold banged her knee against the table as she got up, bit her lip through the pain, and curtsied. The room swayed. "Too easy," she said, lunging for her seat like it was the final round of musical chairs.

"Last night primed you." Eliza licked the grease between her knuckles. "But you're immune."

Roger set aside his whiskey glass; a pair of puny ice cubes bobbed at the surface.

The whisky was a rook, and Marigold moved it straight

toward him. "Pretend it's your wedding."

"Is that what you did last night?" Eliza said. "Did you tip the bartender a fortune too?"

Marigold put a beer to Eliza's mouth. "Take it out on the drink, not your hubby."

She pushed her away. "You trying to break my teeth?"

"Sorry." Her throat felt like a filled-up trash chute. "I had a lot of wi—"

"I'll drink." Roger popped open a beer. He poured at an expert angle, a foamy white cap cresting over the glass. "But let's get to work."

"I printed pages of research." Eliza rubbed the crumbs from her hands and took out a pen and notebook. "You thought the chemical war with laxatives was diabolical? Or your juggling act was acrobatic? Or"—her voice jumped an octave—"your acting was convincing? That was the prelude." She smiled, her teeth a canvas painted with wine. "Slowly, discreetly, we'll poison her from the inside."

"What about witchcraft or Voodoo?" Roger said. Before him, half-chewed nubs of crust littered his cardboard plate like the bones of a devoured animal. "Should we memorize spells too?"

Eliza flipped through the notebook. "I made a note about blood sacrifices somewhere."

Marigold stood, hiding her beer.

"You okay?" Roger asked.

"I'm . . ." She clung to the counter like it was the wall in the deep end of the pool. "Bathroom."

"She'll clean up if anything." Eliza bent over and plucked the napkin from Roger's lap. She wiped her mouth with it. "But tell me, professor. Do you have a better plan?"

The knob shook free from Marigold's grasp; the door slammed. She dumped her beer down the drain. Her reflection tried to catch her eye.

Avoiding the mirror, she dangled her head over the toilet and stuck a finger down her gullet. The running faucet blunted her sounds. Gravity pulled on her insides, but her expulsion system was busted. A net of gooey cheese tangled the vodka, wine, beer, grapefruit juice, and pepperoni inside her. Her coughs were chokingly dry. The grape in the back of her throat was growing, cutting off her windpipe.

She took a vote, the result unanimous, and decided to die. In this bathroom. On the floor or in the shower booth. No one wanted her. No one needed her. And why would they? What could she do? What could she provide?

She closed the sink stopper and let the water fill. When it was deep enough she dove in, mouth open, like she was bobbing for apples.

Gripping the sink, she finally met her reflection. Her wrinkles were aqueducts. Her eyes threatened to slip off her face. Roger and Eliza drank too, but they still looked human.

She swallowed handfuls from the faucet's steam. She wetted a towel and scrubbed away her light makeup.

She breathed.

She told herself these swelling emotions were maudlin facsimiles for real sadness, real loneliness. The end-of-life-as-you-know-it hopelessness you feel when your school crush transfers to another district is not—you realize years later—real heartbreak. But in the moment . . . She was fine. She'd be fine. Time just had to pass.

***

"It needs to be a multifront assault," Roger said, counting the fronts on his fingers.

Eliza caught his hand. "Yeah?"

"We have to balance a reliable long-term plan while taking risks, big swings."

"Can I see your big swing?"

"Stay focused, dear."

Marigold tiptoed in and placed the bottle among the growing number of empties.

"You're alive," Eliza said.

"I was . . . freshening up."

"For your wake?" Eliza twirled the pen. "We're going to play a brainstorming game." She scanned the table. "We have drinks?"

"Lizzie. I'm done," she said, each syllable slippery.

"It's time to work."

Marigold lifted her face to Roger.

His eyes were soft, but he said, "I don't care if you drink, but you have to help us come up with ideas. We're doing this for you."

"She should drink," Eliza said. "That's the game."

"Water then."

"Fine. Ready—for—the—rules? One of us writes. The others drink. When you're done, fold the paper so the next person can't peek." She acted out each instruction like clues in a game of charades. "And Goldie, don't worry. Hit the head whenever you need to. We don't want any accidents."

Fuck you.

Marigold would have said if she had a functioning tongue.

During Eliza's turn, Roger lapped up beer though his wife was only doodling. She added the final period with a flourish and Roger gasped for air. Spittle sprayed the table and dribbled down his chin. He pulled her chair close. "I almost"—he burped into the crook of his elbow, the smell making him wince—"popped."

"I'm making sure you catch up." Eliza licked the slaver from his face, then looked at Marigold. "Your turn."

"Wait." Roger scavenged a slice of veggie hidden beneath a piece of cardboard. As he ate, he cupped a hand under his chin to catch rumpled tomatoes and wilted spinach. When he finished the vegetable runoff, he said, "You're up, Marigold," and waterfalled beer into his glass.

Marigold handled the pen like a piece of alien technology. She scratched out her first words, nicking the table with blue cuts.

Feeling their stares, their eagerness to fly off the starting line, Marigold wrote. And Roger and Eliza drank.

***

Beer warmed. Fingers prodded bellies, checking for bloat. The flow of booze became a trickle, each sip a lash across the palate.

Roger and Eliza played with each other's hair. He squeezed her ear lobe. She rested a hand on his hairy stomach. Marigold laughed along, feigning comprehension of their language of whispers and looks. But those languages only have two fluent speakers and no Rosetta Stone. Even if interpreted, the meaning would be frivolous, not worth the effort of translation, for the meaning exists solely between the two speakers. Would she always be monolingual? Did she even want to learn a new tongue?

"Last round," Eliza said.

While Marigold plagiarized spy movies and the thoughts lurking in the back alleys of her conscience, they finished the backwash in their cups.

"Give me that."

Marigold passed the paper to Eliza.

"We'll let it marinate and review it tomorrow. If we can read it." She creased the paper and dropped it into her handbag. "Where we sleeping, Goldie?"

"Let's call a taxi," Roger said.

"Then we'll have to taxi back for the car."

"Stay," Marigold said. "We're family." She staggered to the foyer. "You know where the guest rooms are."

"Too far." Eliza's hand was down the back of Roger's waistband. "We'll take Todd's room."

"I'll come back tomorrow myself," he said.

"The bedding's washed," Marigold said. "You'll sleep great."

Eliza pulled her husband into the room. "You're offending our host."

"Alright. Goodnight," he said.

Marigold turned toward the stairs.

"Love ya, sis," Eliza said.

"Love—"

The door closed.

17

The hairdryer breathed fire. Marigold lingered over the well-worn pieces hanging in her closet, a perfunctory scan of the menu before selecting her usual. She dressed in loose black pants and a green blouse. Gold earrings. A necklace. She brushed rouge onto her ancient face with the care of an archaeologist.

She felt steady. She had weathered the hangover. For the last two hours—or however long they played the brainstorming game—she pounded water and took frequent bathroom breaks to flush the alcohol from her system and escape the canoodling couple.

Sashaying down the stairs, shoulders back, goosenecked, she presented herself to her prom date—the closed door of Todd's room.

On the front lawn was the newspaper, entombed in plastic, wet with dew. Between advice columns and movie reviews, she took inventory of the fridge. Enough yogurts for all. She made coffee and listened for her sister's elephant stomps and the boyish shuffle of her brother-in-law.

When she was halfway through her first cup, Eliza teetered into the kitchen, pants zipper down, shirt hiked up, her navel exposed. "Come on." She waved her arm like a third base coach imploring her player home. "There he is."

Roger said good morning to the floor. His hair was a poorly kept lawn.

Marigold took the hot mugs out of the microwave.

"You're an angel." Eliza accepted the coffee. "And you"—she kissed Roger's cheek—"you're the devil. You should have seen him, Goldie. His pumping made my heart pump."

Marigold brought over the breakfast. Spoons clattered on the table.

Roger grabbed a yogurt cup. "Thanks."

Eliza clapped. "So last night I was thirsty—it was thirsty work." She suffered through a giggle fit.

Marigold licked the white film off the yogurt lid. "Mm-hmm?"

"This man goes to get me water. Naked, eyes crusted shut, legs bowed like a newborn cow."

"Eliza. Please," Roger said, a speck of yogurt in his stubble.

"You're lucky you're deaf because I was dying of laughter. He was bumping into the furniture, thing-first. With his thing, Goldie. You need to get a wet towel and wipe down every surface in this house." She drank her coffee. "Gosh, I feel good. I feel young. A wild night for us is forgetting to floss our teeth, but last night, we—" Eliza's mug dropped like a gavel. "Oh."

"You alright?" Marigold said.

"Coffee's tunneling through me." She shuffled to the bathroom.

Roger and Marigold reached for the newspaper at the same time. Without looking up, he capitulated.

"You take it," she said.

He pushed the paper toward her.

"Take it."

"I'll read it later," he said.

"You want the sports page? Business? How about the funnies?" She slapped the sections on the table. "Or the Sudoku?" She tore out the puzzle and flung it at him. "Is this it?" she said, forcing herself to whisper.

"You know what Sudoku is."

She shook her head. "Is this it?" The heat intensified through the windows and warmed her legs, itchy under her dark pants. She should stop—stop talking, stop antagonizing. "Is this an eclipse? Am I finally witnessing an eclipse?"

The toilet flushed.

"Marigold." His eyes flashed toward the bathroom.

"Or did I miss it last night? In that room? Tell me."

"Tell you what?" Eliza extracted the Brita from the fridge. "Current events? You're the only event I care about, sis."

Marigold flicked open the style section and covered her face. "We split the paper for a more efficient read." She took a deep breath. "You were quick."

"Gas. I cracked a window." She poured a glass of water. "What was Roger going to tell you?"

"How wonderful you are."

"Sure."

"Your hubby was raving about you." She reconstructed the newspaper, ruffling the pages. "His—"

"Do that later. My head hurts."

She gently stacked the pages on the table. "His analogies are quite poetic."

"Analogies?"

"He's got one for every occasion."

"Okay. Woo me."

Roger cleared his throat and sat up straight. "I . . ." He gulped. "I said—"

"Did you compare this"—she pinched the flab hanging from her arm"—to a warm pillow?"

"I was going to say—"

"You don't live with him, Goldie. His jokes are all inside jokes—with himself. He laughs plenty at least." She snapped her fingers. "Rog, pass me my purse."

He hesitated.

"Rog. The purse."

He handed it over.

"Let's take a gander with sober eyes." She unfolded the paper and ironed out its wrinkles. She drew stars next to promising suggestions. "Wait." Her brow furrowed. "Who wrote this? 'We kill the step-daughter.' Is this a joke? Come on. The only good ideas here"—she smacked the paper"—are my own."

"Your plans," Roger said, "are always the best."

"It's our plan. You can't be half in and half out." She brought the glass to her lips but paused before drinking and said, "This isn't your finance career."

"I'm sorry our life is so hard. God forbid we have to cook most nights."

"Don't take His name in vain. And don't lie. Did you or did you not lead me to believe you would—"

"You think money would make this better?"

"Bait and switch, Rog. Bait and switch."

"We're hungover. We're tired," Marigold said with the droning obligation of a TSA agent chanting: laptop out of the bag, nothing in the pockets, laptop out of the bag, nothing in the pockets. She wanted them to slug it out, wanted Roger to defend himself. But what if he couldn't?

"He's cranky," Eliza said, "because last night it took him a while to find my—"

The doorbell rang.

They froze as if the police had the house surrounded.

Marigold got up uneasily. "I'm sure it's a package."

"A package, eh?" Eliza said. "Is that the nickname for your pool boy?"

"I'll be right back."

The doorbell rang again.

"I have to meet this man," Eliza said. "Come on, Rog."

"Leave me alone," he said.

"We need muscle. Just in case."

"In case what?"

"If it's a big package, you need to carry it. You can handle a big package, can't you?"

18

"Aunt G!" The intruder covered Marigold in limbs, squeezing the breath from her.

A dam burst and chemicals gushed from her brain. Marigold was warm. Awake. Happy. Wendy was here. Right here. Her body. Her soul. Their souls, together, dancing. The missed calls. The empty inbox. Oh, was it worth it. Does food taste this good after a fast? She grabbed her niece like she was a ghost she had to make sure was real, and hugged her harder. Hugging and twisting, almost falling. She held her tight, holding onto this feeling, holding on against time, trying to stall the moving walkway of life pulling them away from this moment. She clasped the black braid crawling down Wendy's back. "It's so long," she said.

"Keeps me warm in the winters."

Eliza surged past them and, dodging the suitcases in the door, retreated to the car.

Marigold wrapped the braid in her hand and counted the knots as if they were rings in a tree. How long had she been gone?

With a soft voice, Roger said, "Is it my turn yet?"

"Dad!"

Father and daughter embraced.

"You're home," he said.

"Astute as ever."

The car horn blared.

"Mom wants you."

"We have to talk, okay?" Roger was misty-eyed.

"I'll be here."

He let go of his daughter and pulled Marigold into a rickety hug. "See you two soon," he said and jogged out to the car.

Wendy unslung her tote bags hanging from her shoulders and stacked them atop her luggage. She started for Todd's room.

"Don't," Marigold said. Your parents fucked on those sheets. "You've graduated to the second floor."

"Finally." She fidgeted. "Did I surprise you?"

"You surprised us all."

"I surprised myself. My work contract ended the same month as my lease. Spent my savings on the flight. Hope you don't mind."

"I've been waiting. Check the mantle."

Wendy swept over the Valentine's Day grams and cards decorated with skinny Christmas trees. On the branches hung shaky silver and gold garland, and plump ornamental balls, misshapen from shoddy crayon work. "The letters I sent you?" She laughed in embarrassment.

"The pool's uncovered too, and," she led her to the kitchen, "I got your favorite."

"I missed these." She tore off the candy wrapper and licked the chili covered mango lollipop.

"I used to hide these from your mom. She said they'd give you stomach cancer."

Wendy touched the tip of her tongue.

"Does it taste the same?" Marigold asked.

"It's . . . sharp. How old are these?"

Marigold searched the bag for an expiration date. "Well . . . you should've visited sooner."

"How soon? I'm licking a barnacle."

"Uh." She tossed the bag in the trash. "Three years ago."

Laughing, they moseyed into the backyard. Kickboards leaned against the house like loitering teenagers. Stiff, uncooked pool noodles were strewn behind planter boxes.

Wendy rolled up her pants and untied her boots. Sock indentations wrapped her foot like an ankle monitor. Black lint was trapped in her toenails. "Aunt G." She dangled her feet over the edge of the pool. "I missed this." She dunked her legs in the water and squealed like a child.

Marigold sat at the shaded patio table, tracing circles on a dusty bottle of sunblock. "Your work contract ended?"

"I chose not to renew."

"Your dad bragged about you making it in PR. Meeting celebrities."

"That was fun for a while, but it's hard to be fake. On-line. In-person. I can't do it." She stripped out of her flannel shirt and let the straps of her tank top fall off her shoulders. "You still play the ukulele?"

"I donated it. It was a silly hobby."

"But you were so good."

"It was time to retire."

"What about the towels? Are they still in the basket?"

"They might be as rough as those lollipops."

Wendy grabbed one, dried her feet, and ambled into the house.

A neighbor's garage door rattled shut. Buzzing bees commuted to the Sweet Alyssum flowers nestled in bunches, in prefabricated bouquets, where two butterflies danced together like nervous preteens. Marigold stuck her arm out and the sun tasted her.

Balancing a cell phone, spoon, and a bowl of cereal, Wendy emerged in a faded black bikini. She hip-checked the sliding door shut and approached carefully.

"Cute swimsuit," Marigold said.

Hearing the compliment, Wendy busted into a strut, swinging her hips with such force that milk sloshed out from the bowl. She parked at the table.

"The heat will turn that into soup."

"I could've been a competitive eater." Wendy leaned over her breakfast and guzzled down the cereal. When she finished, she spooned pool water into the bowl, rinsed it clean, and dried it with her flannel.

Marigold watched her niece's ingenuity without comment.

Wendy scrolled through her phone and placed it in the bowl. A bustling, festive beat reverberated from the makeshift speaker. Slinking into the water, she said, "You going to join me? I flew all this way."

Marigold trundled over, planted her feet on the top step of the pool stairs, and shuddered.

"Cold?"

"Perfect." Marigold shielded her eyes from the sunlight flashing off the water. Her pants stuck to her calves like postage stamps. "We didn't use this pool enough."

"We had barbecues. You and dad played deep-sea diver with me."

"Deep-sea diver?"

"With the weighted rings."

"We called that fetch. It wasn't enough."

"Uncle Todd didn't like kids much, huh? He disappeared every time I came over."

Marigold glanced around. He wasn't there of course. "Uncle Todd didn't like people."

"Then what drew you to him?"

"His money."

She splashed her aunt. "Come on. It's us."

"That's why I'm being honest."

"What did he look like when he was young?"

"You've seen pictures."

"I want you to describe him."

Her mind drifted across lanes, deciding which exit to take. She righted the wheel. "He shrunk as he got older, but . . ." She struck a bodybuilding pose.

"Say it."

"He was . . . muscular—he played water polo and swam in high school. And he had the cutest nose," Marigold said. "He had the best of both worlds really—a pretty face and a hard body."

"Gross." She swam over and rested her head on Marigold's thigh. "Tell me more."

"His hair was"—she coiled Wendy's braid around her wrist—"like yours. I'm the reason he went bald. I petted him so much." Shortly after the wedding, his genes fizzled and his hair fell out in tufts.

Wendy coughed. Snot poked out from one of her nostrils. "It's sweet how you remember him."

"You're getting soft in your old age." Marigold dabbed at Wendy's eyes like a cutman trying to keep the swelling down. "Should we pick another song? Something less cheery?" The crowd chanted in Portuguese, begging the band for an encore.

"Let it play." Wendy dove down, did a handstand, toppled over. She came up for air and hopped on the ledge, her tears replaced with pool water. "You met in college, right?"

"Yes."

"Did you have class together? Was he an unprofessional TA preying on a helpless underclassman?"

She laughed. "So detailed."

"Am I right?"

"We met at a party."

"Did he invite you?"

"He found me."

"He chose you."

"Maybe. It was dark." The first night they had met

their sweat-slicked foreheads were pressed together. A bean burrito thickened his breath while vodka sharpened hers. He invaded her with bombarding lips and tunneling hands as she futilely searched his pockets for a pack of gum.

"So," Wendy said. "You met at a party and started dating?"

On weekends, they had drunk and danced and smoked. And in the mornings they exchanged ice breaker questions—What's your major? Where you from?—while she gathered her clothes from the floor. "More or less."

"You got married young."

"Younger than you are now."

"How did you know he was the one?"

"The one?"

"Don't scoff. How did you decide to get married?"

"We all wanted it." Marigold slid her legs further into the water. "Your mom planned brunches and picnics with his parents. Even then, Todd was serious. Your grandma and mom were attracted to that. And his family . . ."

"They loved you?"

She nodded. They loved Eliza. The saleswoman. Who

sold Todd's parents on the promise of perfect offspring. To hear her say it, the tantrum-throwing toddlers they encountered at the Hazard Center Mall were inferior prototypes to the beautiful angels Todd and Marigold would produce.

"How did he pop the question? Was it extravagant like in a hot air balloon? Or was it San Diegan?"

"San Diegan?"

"On a tandem bike or while building a sandcastle?"

Todd's mother had drunkenly suggested it at a holiday dinner. Toasts were made. Eliza volunteered to plan the wedding—an idea met with enthusiastic agreement. Momentum trapped Marigold to an assembly line, where she was put together with parts she didn't want. Eliza and her future mother-in-law shuttled her to vendors. They stuffed her full of cake, suffocated her with gardenias, and escorted her to church to pray the rosary and receive fertility blessings.

Wendy balled her fist and stuck it in her aunt's face. "Say it into the mic."

"He wouldn't want me to—."

"He won't know, but fine. Let me guess." She thought for a moment. "Considering your age at the time . . . You were in Pacific Beach . . . at a dingy restaurant."

"Thanks."

"Dingy in a well-used way. Like a broken-in baseball glove. A burger place! He put the ring in your milkshake."

"Sounds romantic." Marigold recalled the studio apartment they had lived in before Todd got his inheritance. Every night they fried eggs or boiled pasta and had sex. Had that been romantic?

"Thank you, your honor. No further questions." She dropped into the water and doggie-paddled to the end of the pool.

"Those YMCA lessons paid off."

"Change and hop in. We can race."

"I'll drown."

"In the event of an emergency." Wendy waded to the shallow end. Her belly button was stitched above the water like the sun over the horizon. "Stand up."

"Bathtubs are lethal for me now."

"I know mouth to mouth."

Marigold pointed to her hearing aids. "I'll electrocute

us. What would the pool guy think? Besides." She grabbed an armful of beach towels from the basket, piled them by the ledge, and took her place atop the cushioned throne. "This is a spectator sport."

"Fine. Spectate then." Pushing off the wall, Wendy floated on her back. The neighbor's lemon tree waved in the breeze. The grill cover rippled.

"I want to see the seasons change," Marigold said.

"It is beautiful. The first year. But you learn to appreciate the springs and falls. I don't want to appreciate the weather for half the year." Wendy ducked below the surface and popped up, spouting water from her mouth. "I want to be spoiled."

"The weather's too perfect here. It feels fake."

"See? You're spoiled."

"You do like it over there, right?"

"Sure. But it's not home." Wendy rattled off her Christmas list of restaurants, beaches, and friends she wanted to visit.

"What about all those adventures with your roommate?"

"She's . . . swell." Wendy laughed. "But I miss real friends."

"We got plenty of cars. Go see them."

She swam to Marigold and gripped her foot. "You'd be a great mom."

"Because I'll let you take a car? Stop—that tickles."

She squeezed her aunt's foot. "Dad told me."

"Whatever he said—don't listen to him. He lives in the rumor mill."

"He told me you couldn't have kids."

"Don't need 'em. I got you."

"Did you have names picked out?"

"I had one I liked. Olivia. But I'd call her Olive." How long had it been since she thought of that name?

"Cousin Olive."

She expected Wendy to cry again, but her niece climbed out of the pool and yanked a pink towel out from under Marigold's butt. Bunny ear-looped bikini bottom strings rested like slugs in secretion. With cadaverous stillness, she lay atop a field of flamingos. The sun consumed the moisture streaking her body.

"Let me see a cannonball," Marigold said.

"Members of the audience may get wet."

"I'm here to see a show."

Wendy moonwalked to the grill and launched into her approach like a gymnast, her scream bigger than the splash.

19

The days tumbled by. Inspired by cooking blogs, Wendy whipped up cannellini bean casseroles and tuna omelets. For their ritual nightcap, they dressed the patio table for a seance and played candlelit crazy eights and kings in the corner, wedging their cards under wine glass paperweights.

They took the Mustang by the beach. Parents put earphones in and sunglasses on, shirking their parental responsibilities one sense at a time. Unashamed fathers shifted their blubber to get an even crisp. Applied lotion disappeared in crevices. Wendy wore her new orange and pink swimsuit. She played tag with the tide, while Marigold burrowed her toes into the sand and giggled when the water rushed past her ankles.

***

Wendy was a faster driver than her father. It wasn't just the speed. To her, the GPS was gospel, while Roger opted for circuitous scenic routes.

"You trying to rip out the airbag?" Wendy said.

Marigold took her hands off the dashboard. "It's a habit."

"I'm a universal donor. You're safe next to me."

"Isn't that one of your dad's jokes?"

"He's the universal receiver." Her voice broke a bit. "He brags he can get blood delivered."

"I hear that every Monday."

Wendy sniffled.

"Cold?"

She changed lanes. "You should renew your license."

"I have to take the test again."

"We can practice at a cemetery. That's where dad taught me. You can't hurt anybody."

Stopped at a red light, Marigold checked out the pedestrians checking out Wendy. At restaurants too, she had noticed waiters scanning for flaws in the structural integrity of her shirts. The light turned green. "To the theater, please," Marigold said.

For their biweekly matinee thriller, they arrived in the Mercedes SUV. Marigold bought popcorn and Milk Duds supplemented with the ticket savings from her senior discount. They filed into a row, two-thirds up—the best seats in the house according to Wendy. A large man, cactus needles of hair sticking out from his nose and ears, stood to let them pass.

During the movie, Wendy wiped her buttery, salty, chocolatey fingers on the seat cushion. At the climactic rooftop standoff, she missed her mouth entirely and a landslide of popcorn rumbled down her chest and into her lap.

Afterward they drove to a cafe for coffee and tiramisu. Though the weather didn't meet San Diego standards, they sat outside. The grated picnic table cast a honeycomb shadow over their feet. Marigold snuggled in her cardigan, while Wendy, protesting sleeves, rubbed the goosebumps bubbled on her arms.

"Sorry, I'm being rude." Wendy set her phone down and sipped her vanilla macchiato.

"Writer's block?"

"It's this guy."

Marigold had noticed Wendy—while watching TV and before starting the car—smiling at her phone. "Special?"

"When I look at him, I have to remind myself to blink."

Marigold silenced the alarm bells ringing inside her. Love was blinding, so let her be blinded. "What do you want to say?"

"I don't know."

Wendy explained modern dating, defined terminology—with examples—and complained about having to juggle multiple partners to hedge against rejection.

"I hear you," Marigold said. "And I don't want to dismiss what you're saying, but . . ."

"Dismiss it. Please."

"What's his name?"

"Ben."

"Say—give it." Marigold took the phone but kept typing Ven instead of Ben.

"Didn't you have a cell phone for a while?"

"I don't trust these tracking devices."

"You're the only person I know with a landline."

"It's an heirloom." Marigold gave the phone to her niece. "This contraption is so unromantic. You do it. Ready?"

"I can't believe my aunt is ghostwriting my texts."

"Say: Ben I'm starving but I'm picky and I only want you."

Wendy wrote out the message.

"Let me see . . . Zoom in. No zoom? And this is the latest technology? Get rid of the commas—the run-on makes it urgent. Okay, good. Send it."

"Now?"

"Before you change your mind."

"Sent."

"Turn it off. He'll be on the next flight out."

She stuffed her phone into her purse along with their unused napkins. "I should have known you'd be good at this."

"How dare you." Marigold grinned. "I was with one man for 40 years."

"I've seen the pictures. Even in the hazy photographs, you glow. Mom hated when I went through those albums. She acted like she caught me playing with a gun." She stacked their cups and crushed the straw wrappers in her fist. "Ready to go back to school?"

"If it's on your list."

"Show me what I missed out on."

"What was your bullshit reason for transferring again?" Marigold stroked her chin. "You wanted to see the seasons change?"

"Dad believed it."

"Of course he did. He was humoring you."

20

Stuck at a stop sign, they waited as students poured out from McDonald's cupping iced coffees and dangling French fries from their lips. Their backward-hatted heads joined the pedestrian caravan blocking traffic. Wendy turned left. They passed the taco stand where Marigold had layered salsa onto her burritos like a monk laboring over a sand mandala. Did she ever eat there sober?

They parked and entered the campus.

They walked over the fossils buried in Marigold's memory. Through the Mediterranean garden where she and a girlfriend had, celebrating the end of finals, drank champagne from plastic cups and gotten tipsy on empty stomachs.

"Does it look the same?" Wendy asked.

Marigold updated her mental map of the school as she encountered the renovated student center, the bike lane, and the vegetarian restaurant. "There's more trash cans."

Despite the changes, students still lounged around the turtle pond, heads propped on backpacks, reviewing notes and scratching the grass itch. Skateboarders skirted the campus police with familiar nonchalance. In the bowling alley, fifth-year seniors still pummeled pins while exchange students crowded around TVs and cheered on their soccer teams in half a dozen languages. The president's statue was the same shade of burnt oatmeal. Finding things in the same place made her nostalgic—like opening a time capsule—and validated—like remembering where she put her sunglasses.

Wendy peppered her aunt with questions about classes, teachers, study habits. Marigold fielded them with the ease of an astrophysicist in a planetarium.

"You ever see your college chums?" Wendy asked.

They drifted apart like pieces of ice cracked off a glacier. The ones who stayed plastered San Diego Chargers stickers to their cars and only left the county for the occasional bachelorette party in Tijuana. "Only for a bit."

"That's sad"

"They had families. Kids. It's hard."

"That will never happen to me."

Marigold thought of her friends, and the goodwill they had stockpiled over the course of their friendship. Had that goodwill expired? If she called them now, would their conversations be stiff from disuse? Had they sent sympathy cards when Todd died?

A woman in jeans, boots, and a knitted scarf scurried

past them.

"Is it that cold for a scarf?" Marigold said.

"Hickeys."

"I need proof."

"Look."

The woman picked up her pace and jumped into the arms of a beanie-capped, bearded man. They kissed like they were saying goodbye at the airport.

"We're a territorial species," Wendy said. "Hickeys mark new romance." She saddled up beside her aunt. "Did you ever wear a scarf on campus? Where did Uncle Todd take you to—you know?"

"Eat?"

"To fool around."

Todd called them love bites. And he branded her with them into her forties. Biting, sucking, and twisting the skin of her neck, wrists, and thighs. "Do you ask your mother these questions?"

"Like she would answer."

They plopped down on a bench facing the library. A

group of basketball players lumbered by, decked in red and black, SDSU stamped on the chests and down the legs of their sweatsuits.

"Are you planning to see her?" Marigold said.

"Already did."

"That first day doesn't count."

"Shit."

Cursing was sweet coming from her.

"We can all get together," Marigold said, trying to sound genuine.

"I'll see dad."

"Your mom might want to talk."

"I don't care. I avoid her for a reason. I moved across the country for a reason." A pigeon pecked at a weed growing from between two concrete slabs. "She lies. And denies it when you confront her. She makes it seem like it's your fault for knowing the truth."

"Okay."

"Mom didn't tell me your husband died. Why didn't she tell me?"

"She was busy. She had to take care of everything be-cause I . . ."—was boxing his stuff and hunting for homes in Vermont—"couldn't."

"Let's have a barbecue." Wendy tugged on her aunt's arm. "Dad will grill and I'll rent a karaoke machine and we can play fetch."

"Okay." Her last night in the house. The send-off. She would gorge herself on meat and crack bawdy jokes. She'd swim naked. Sing a duet with her niece. They'd make a big mess. And when Roger and Wendy fell asleep, all happy and warm, she'd take a hot shower, or, if she was feeling dra-matic, draw a bath. Let the faucet run. Simmering in the tub with her book, she'd swallow a sleeping pill and a sip of vodka sour each time she turned a page. She'd stay there till the sleep came, the water running over onto the tile. She just hoped to finish the story first. "That'd be nice."

Students emerged from class like bees in smoke, but soon they began to buzz, swarm, fly off in clusters.

Wendy was crying. "I'm so soft." Napkins fell from her purse. She bent down and picked them up.

"Don't use those—you'll get pink eye." Marigold opened her glasses case. "Here."

Wendy took the micro-fiber cloth. "You wear glasses?"

"I lend them to your dad so he can make out the per-unit prices. And I use them to read my lottery numbers."

Wendy admired the floral design. "I'll ruin it."

"So ruin it."

She blew bubbles of snot into the cloth. When her eyes dried, they floated in a stream of students back to the parking structure, where the machine robbed them of their coins. Before departing, Wendy shot off a round of text messages.

Evening settled in; drivers folded sun visors and rolled up windows. Traffic squeezed through accidents on both shoulders like fluid from an IV drip.

"It's going to be a while," Wendy said. "Sleep."

"You're the kid." Marigold yawned. "I'm the adult. You should be curled up in the back."

"Will you carry me to bed how dad used to?"

"We had a big day." She reclined her seat. "A movie. Fancy cafe. A tour of my alma mater."

"I cried."

"You cried." She closed her eyes. "See? You're still the kid."

"Rest."

"I'm just sleep talking. I've slept so good since you came. Like a dog that gets a long walk every day."

"Don't say that."

"I'm the kid then. Zapped of energy. Tuckered out. Pooped."

"So sleep."

Wendy roused her aunt when they pulled into the driveway. "Your school made me miss my friends." The engine was running. "I'm going to stay out for a bit."

Marigold exited the car. "Why don't you have a slumber party like old times?"

"I'll be back soon," Wendy said. "They have jobs to go to tomorrow."

Marigold kicked her shoes toward the closet. Both shots missed wide; the latter clanged off the door frame.

In her bedroom, she unbuttoned her shirt, wrestled her socks off, and fell back into bed, her shirt coming apart like a window curtain. The ceiling fan resembled Eliza's necklace—cross-shaped and wooden.

She dumped her hearing aids on the nightstand next

to the Peter Cameron novel. One had a hair on it, cemented in ear wax. Her cleaning kit was downstairs, so she opened the book and set it down like a teepee over the hearing aids.

She tongued a piece of popcorn wedged in her teeth. She almost had it too when the phone rang.

21

Was it Roger pressuring her to go grocery shopping? Or was it Wendy? Asking if she wanted an order of pad see ew.

The phone rang.

Maybe Betty had spotted a clerical error and the house was hers after all. Or maybe every single one of her in-laws had dropped dead with brain aneurysms. Could it be that for the first time in her life, perhaps in history, her problems died when she ignored them. Maybe, just maybe she could cancel that barbecue send-off.

"Hello," Marigold said.

"Is she there?"

"Lizzie?"

"Is she there?"

"Your daughter? She's with friends. She'll be back—"

"Does she know about Todd?"

"That he's dead?"

"About the inheritance?" Eliza said.

"I didn't bring it up."

"That's the truth?"

"No. I'm lying."

"Roger said he didn't tell her either."

"Fascinating."

"We're coming over."

"Not tonight."

"I figured out the next part of the plan. You'll be the star. Like at Jasmine's."

"Tell me now."

"Can't share this over the phone."

"Then let's wait till tomorrow."

"You know how stubborn Roger is. We're already on our way."

Marigold changed and marched down the stairs, the train of her bathrobe dragging on the steps. On her feet were bear slippers, a gag gift from Wendy. She fanned herself with the refrigerator door. Each time she peered in she found the same half onion, the same tub of minced garlic.

The clichés came to mind. She was in a fog, a daze. Exhausted. Old. She stripped these words of their letters and sounds and gathered their meanings bare, bundled them up, doused them in anger, and used them as kindling to light a fire inside her.

When the spark didn't catch, she settled on sliced cucumbers.

She munched at the counter. The juicer's parts, coated with an orange glaze, soaked in the sink. They had sworn to clean up later when they had more energy.

A mouth-breathing engine clammed up, doors slammed, an elephant stomped, and a boy dragged his feet. Marigold's mind was a wet paper bag, unable to hold anything of weight. Excitement and fear floated by, but she didn't reach for them. She didn't feel them. As Eliza entered the dining room, a thought struck her: Drunk drivers survive accidents because they don't brace for impact.

22

"Look at these models," Eliza said. Wendy and Marigold's senior portraits were pinned to the fridge. "So vain." She placed a Big Apple magnet between Wendy's eyes. "Thanks for dressing up for us."

Marigold shoved her hands into the pockets of her robe. "Late notice." She tucked her bear-slippered feet under the chair, out of sight. The dishwasher's drawbridge hung down. On the table in a lacquer bowl was a ball pit of citrus: cuties, grapefruits, lemons, and oranges. "Best I could do."

Eliza swabbed the tabletop and inspected her palm "Keeping up with the pup?"

"Barely," Marigold said.

"What have you been up to?" Roger said.

"Everything. Wendy took pictures with her phone. She—"

"When's she leaving?" Eliza's roar was that of a caged animal—unsettling but not dangerous.

"Haven't asked," Marigold said.

"She brought big suitcases. Maybe she's moving back. She wouldn't be the first. How many have left, Goldie? But they always come back." Eliza took an orange, sniffed it, and threw it back in the bowl. "Bet you can't wait till she leaves though. You look tired."

"I look how I feel."

"I'm tired too."

Eliza's frown was an infinite parabola. Her turkey wattle descended like a scrotum.

"Take a guest room," Marigold said. "Sleep."

"Can't. I'm preoccupied—Roger says I'm obsessed. But you appreciate my effort, don't you?" She glanced at her husband, who stared at the table. "You think I'm obsessed, Goldie?"

"I can't think." Marigold tapped her temple. "Brain's not working."

"Can you get it working? I didn't tell him the plan because you freaked out last time." Her voice had lost its bite but, like a diluted cocktail, it still packed heat. "Rog, sweetie, get me a drink. And a beverage for our hostess. She needs one. Why else would she forget to offer us refreshments?"

Roger got up. "A drink drink?"

"I'm fine," Marigold said. "There's beer in the crisper."

"Juice." Eliza eyed the counter. On it was the food pusher, blasted with orange guts. "You have juice, right?"

"We can make more."

"Too much work. What else you got?"

"Sparkling water."

"That crap makes me feel old."

"We got the Brita."

"Sparkling then," Eliza said. "I want flavor."

Roger arranged the coasters.

"I've been thinking." Eliza nipped her strawberry water. "Todd never let you drive."

"I drove," Marigold said. "At the beginning."

"He didn't leave you anything."

"I don't need reminding."

"Doesn't that infuriate you? Don't you want to floor one of his precious cars full-throttle into his headstone?" She pulled out her notebook and flipped to a page. City blocks sketched in pencil. At an intersection, a stick figure was scratched out in red. "Pick a car. The SUV is high up—claim you didn't see her—and sturdy, so you'll be safe."

"What is this?" Roger said.

Eliza's voice picked up speed. "Be the distraught, dementia-ridden old lady they think you are. Be who Allan thinks you are. It's simple." She circled the stick figure. "We'll follow the step-daughter—"

"You're fuckin' crazy," Roger said

"Pretend it's Allan. Pretend it's Todd. Pretend it's me—I don't care."

Red lashes obscured the stick figure's eyes, nose, and mouth. Marigold couldn't picture the step-daughter's real face or remember her name. "Do I confirm the kill?"

"Jar her insides is all."

"She'll go to prison," Roger said.

"This was your idea."

"I was joking."

"We can't let that bastard win."

"We'll sue him. Betty will help."

"What? "

"Betty will find something on him."

"Who are you talking about?"

"Allan."

"Allan? Have you been paying attention? Not Allen. No. Todd. Todd is the—"

The front door slammed shut. They heard the metallic splash of keys dropped in a bowl of coins.

"You said she was out with friends," Eliza whispered.

"Sorry," Marigold said. Wendy had seen her father's car of course. Would she sneak up the stairs or—

"Having a reunion without me?" Wendy shouted from the foyer.

She strode in, hugged Roger, and offered Marigold a sip of her bubble tea. "It's Jasmine, your favorite."

Marigold chewed the tapioca balls slowly but, like a condemned inmate eating their last meal, the impending uncertainty prevented her from tasting anything.

The chair across from Eliza was vacant.

Wendy stood.

"Marigold says you've taken pictures of your time at home?" Roger said.

Wendy licked the foam off the straw, set the cup on the table, and took her phone out from her butt pocket.

"We should hit a Padres game," he said after cycling through the photos.

"I'd love that."

"And we'd love to hear how you've been. Right, dear?" He put his arm around Eliza. "So how's it being home? Has it changed at all?"

"The radio only plays five songs like it always has," she said, "but the songs are different. You know what I mean? It's different but not really."

"Well it's better with you here. So New York. How was—"

"Cute drawing," Wendy said.

Eliza snapped the notebook shut.

"Show me your art."

"Your aunt and I were talking. Before you interrupted."

"About what?"

Eliza took the bubble tea cup to the sink. "Leaving

your trash wherever you please." She rinsed it on full blast and placed it in the drying rack. "This isn't your home."

Wendy strolled to where her mom was. "Aunt G." She threw the cup in the recycling bin. "What were you talking about?"

Marigold shifted. "Nothing."

"Don't be nosy," Eliza said. Water had sprayed her white shirt; it resembled a Rorschach inkblot.

"Dad. What were they talking about?"

"Nothing important," Roger said.

"Then tell me."

"Mind your business." Eliza went back to her seat and grabbed a lemon from the bowl.

"It's unhealthy to have so many secrets, mother."

"Secrets protect people."

"But the truth will—"

"You squawked as a baby and you're squawking now." She crushed the lemon; its juice dripped down her fingers. "If you're so curious, so thirsty for knowledge, here's a fun fact, daughter." She sounded like a game show host. "Did you know your dad didn't want you?"

Wendy stared at Eliza.

"Yup. He made the appointment. He begged them to pry you out of me. But I refused. You're alive because of me." She pressed her glistening thumb to her chest. "Not him. Not your aunt. Me."

23

Roger's tears made Wendy cry.

"I was scared," he said. The wrinkles on his forehead—straight like lines on notebook paper—were darker, bolder, traced in blank ink.

"Dad—"

"I was young. I didn't want to accept it."

"—I know." She wiped her eyes with the back of her wrist.

He studied her.

"Remember how I donated blood senior year?"

He laughed weakly. "You wanted to ditch class and eat free donuts."

She touched his face. "I'm O negative. The universal donor. Like mom. So I can't be—you can't be my—"

"You know?"

"Of course she knows," Eliza said. "She ambushed me, screaming about alleles and—"

"That's why you left." It wasn't a question. He pulled Wendy into his lap. "The day you were born was the day

I stopped caring. It didn't matter if your mother didn't love me. It didn't matter if you weren't my blood. I held you, touched your eyelids, your fingernails. Felt your tiny breaths." He was steadier now. "I held you like a bomb because if you had cried . . . Crying would've been rejection—proof you'd never be mine. But when the nurse reached for you, I asked for more time. In that moment all I wanted, in my whole life, was to be there, holding you." He smiled at the memory. "And I knew then . . . only your love had to be mine. And that's always been enough."

Wendy wrapped her arms around him and together they cried, heaving like a ship in rough seas.

"Of course it was enough." Eliza got up and washed her hands. "Compared to your real father."

Wendy peeled away from Roger's shoulder, looping tear-soaked hairs pressed into her cheeks. "What?" Her voice was shattered from crying.

"You do want to know, right? You both do."

"I . . . I need air." Wendy darted to the door, slid the screen open, and hurried into the yard. Roger trailed her.

"It is a lovely night." Eliza gripped her sister's arm so hard she could've measured her blood pressure. "She needs our support."

From Marigold's angle, all she saw out the door was black sky. "Right."

"Wait." Eliza looked her up and down. "I just realized something."

"What?"

"It can wait. A bit."

They loaded up on beers and stepped through the black portal.

24

Drunk moths fluttered about the porch light. The pool skimmer nibbled on a kickboard. A cloying lavender scent wafted from the patio table, where Wendy stared at a sloping candle as if pondering a birthday wish.

"You like beer, Wendy?" Eliza sat next to Marigold. The sphere of candlelight illuminated the tabletop, but under the giant patio umbrella, darkness devoured their limbs, their skin, and left them only their shadows and voices. "We should drink. We'll need it."

"You need an opener," Roger said.

"I got it." She twisted the bottle cap with the sleeve of Marigold's bathrobe. "Come on, you mother—"

"You need an opener."

She pretended to bite the cap off, growling. She smiled. No one laughed. She gave up on the beer and was silent for a while. The candle shrunk. When she spoke again, she said, "I know you'll forgive me."

Wendy looked away.

"You're a woman now," Eliza said. "You've been torn. Tempted. Mistaken. We're all selfish. You've been selfish before, right? Once?" She nodded. "Yeah, you'll forgive me.

But you."

Roger sat up straight. He grabbed Wendy's hand and said to her, "Nothing will change."

"Good to know," Eliza said. "Todd's the father."

Roger knocked the bottles over like bowling pins. "Todd?" Purple wax oozed from the overturned candle.

"But isn't her love enough?" Eliza said.

"Todd?" he said again. "Your church buddy?"

Wendy hugged and patted him as if he were on fire, smothering the flames before they left him unrecognizable.

Eliza shrugged. "He wasn't special. If you're worried about that. But he didn't need a 45-minute shower before-hand to perform either."

Roger hid behind the slender waterfall of Wendy's braid. On the table, the melted wax was beginning to harden. It reminded Marigold of the frozen pebbles sliding across Jasmine's floor.

"Why do you think I was here all the time?" Eliza said. "To feed him? Watch his boring game shows? You think I enjoyed his jaundice hands groping my thighs? Please. I had to make sure he was going to give me what he promised."

She motioned to the pool, the house. "I kept his secret. And yeah, he kept mine. But I had more to lose. And what did I gain?" She swung at a moth that had flown too close. "God knows he didn't pay child support."

Marigold followed the insect flitting above her sister. *Where do the butterflies sleep?* she wondered. *Do they sleep at all?*

"You don't care, do you, Goldie? It wasn't love. And I wasn't unique." She laughed. "We should start a support group: The Women Unsatisfied by Toddrick Barton. We might actually make some friends."

Moths came from cocoons, Marigold knew, and butterflies from a chrysalis. But what happens to the caterpillars that die mid-metamorphosis? Are there autopsies? How are the obituaries written? Is it: *This caterpillar lived a long life,* or *this butterfly was taken too soon?*

"Even at the end he wanted me," Eliza said. "He wanted me to—you know how he was, Goldie. He had a hunger and didn't understand the word no. It didn't mean anything. We didn't mean anything to him. He told me once. To my face. He said you were more fun to look at, but I was more fun to be inside of." She sank back and pressed a cold beer to her neck. Quivering, she said, "Okay. Your turn, sis. No more secrets."

Marigold's fingernail pierced a glob of warm wax, smooth like sea glass.

"Be honest." Her skin absorbed the bottle's condensation. Eliza set it down. "I'll understand. We're more alike than you know. We'll be closer now. And if it's not true, deny it. Come on. Deny it. It's easy. Repeat after me: I didn't fuck your husband. Go ahead. Try. You can do it. Nice and slow. I—didn't—fuck—your—husband."

"Leave her alone," Wendy said.

She snatched Marigold's wrist. "We shared clothes. A bed. Men. I tasted yours and you tasted mine. We're square. At least we quit decades ago. I served my penance. I'm absolved. But you two . . . with your trips to the grocery store. Every Monday, right?"

"Nothing happened." Roger stared Eliza down though she held a knife to the neck of his masculinity.

"You just slept on the couch? You just watched the sunset—"

"They're not like you," Wendy said.

"You don't know shit."

"They couldn't be like you. You're a cheater and a liar."

Eliza sneered, then laughed warmly. "Rog. I'm having an . . . an epiphany. You were right. You were right all along. I should have aborted her."

"You—"

"How does it feel? Neither of your fathers wanted you and now I regret it."

"I—"

"And you think you know her? Your sweet Aunt G." Eliza swiped at Marigold's face and pinched her earlobe. "Ring the Pope." She drove a finger into her sister's ear. "You can hear? You'll be canonized within the week."

25

Her brain commanded her to protect her ears, shove Eliza, and unleash the feelings stewing in the stagnant sewers of her heart. Marigold opened her mouth but couldn't translate her fury into words. They wouldn't get it. To them, Todd was a run-of-the-mill asshole. Of course, Roger and Wendy would listen and say they understood. Understood what she had done and why she'd done it. They'd be empathetic. But empathy has its limits. People never just listen—they judge. They'd leave her for good—leave her to rot.

Marigold closed her mouth. Her breath tasted of stale popcorn. A bulletin scrolled across the news ticker of her mind: Drunk drivers survive accidents because they don't brace for impact.

Her hand stayed on the table, chipping at the wax.

"You performed plenty of miracles," Eliza said. "No kids though I know Todd never used rubb—Oh, wait. That's right." She jabbed at her sister's stomach. "How many miscarriages did you have? And the doctors never found anything wrong?"

When their mother had worked nights, Marigold tried to stay up until she returned to the apartment. She swept her drowsy arm like a white cane across the bed, searching for her sleeping mother. One night, with Eliza snoring, Marigold was awake when the floorboards whined. She sat up in greeting but froze. She screamed at the creature in the doorway, way too tall with cement skin, smudged cheekbones, and sea anemone tentacles sprouting from her eyes.

"She had a D&C for Christ's sake," Roger said.

"Did she?" Eliza said. "I didn't go with her. Neither did Todd. Did you?"

"She . . . took a taxi—she insisted."

"You won't let her go grocery shopping alone, and you didn't ask how it went? The procedure requires anesthesia. They tell you to have someone there."

"She didn't bring it up. And I . . . I didn't pry."

"Then Todd gets sick," Eliza said, shredding through his rationalization. "And again, the doctors were baffled."

From then on, Marigold had pretended to be asleep. Through squinted eyes, she watched her mother peel out of her stockings and untangle herself from intricate tops. She used the bathroom for a while. And when she came out, she kissed Marigold on the forehead, her lips warm and dry. Her face smelled of soap and perfume. Lotion made her skin sticky. Sometimes when her mom massaged her feet, her hair would slip into the space between her toes and tickle her. Marigold had to bite her lips to keep from squirming, it tickled so bad.

"He wanted a divorce; he told me. But you didn't sign a postnup, remember? I convinced him you were docile. That he had nothing to worry about. And he's dead now." She paused for a moment, reflecting on the fact. "Because of me, this house is yours. And you do deserve it, Goldie. You went through so much. Trapped in this prison. Having everything you needed, but nothing you wanted."

Marigold swallowed and held her blinks. She focused on the memory of her mother checking if her daughters were asleep as she stuffed her work clothes behind the dresser.

"But it's Wendy's house," Roger said.

"What?" Wendy said.

They didn't notice Marigold was crying. She considered sobbing. Instead, she admired the purple bits of wax under her fingernails.

"Your fa—Todd left everything to his firstborn," Roger said. "That's you."

"Aunt G?"

Her niece's broken stare bore into her skull. The desperation in her plea made Marigold wish she was deaf. She wanted to give Wendy a signal, or least comfort her. But her hands, her wrinkled hands, demanded her attention.

"Aunt G, is it true?"

"Because of me." Eliza shot up. Her head knocked against the umbrella. "I'm the reason you're alive. I'm the reason this house is yours. I'm your mother." She grabbed her daughter's arm. "After all I did for him, he wanted me to suffer. He thought you hated me. But there's no hate in your heart." She petted Wendy's braid. "You're different from him. You're . . . sweet and—"

Would she ever stop talking? Marigold closed her eyes, locked them shut, and wobbled like a fussy toddler in a high chair.

"Aunt G!"

"She's faking it," Eliza said. "Sorry, sis. You're too old for Julliard."

The ground was cool against Marigold's cheek, but her bathrobe blanket kept her warm.

Roger felt along her neck. "Has she been sick?"

"She's tired some days, and"—Wendy glanced at Eliza—"I found sleeping pills in her bathroom."

"Let's get her to the car."

Eliza's breath pelted Marigold's forehead. "This was your plan, wasn't it?"

"Get away from her," Wendy said.

"Grab the legs." Roger's hands slid under her armpits. "No, the knees. On three. Ready? One, two, three."

Marigold levitated. Her head lolled against his gut.

"You want to steal my family," Eliza said.

They struggled through the door. The kitchen smelled of citrus.

Wendy refastened her grip. "I need a break."

"Can you make it to the couch?" Roger said.

They laid Marigold to rest. Her face twinged, inundated with saltwater. Someone dug through loose change. A car alarm echoed into the night.

"I know you can hear me," Eliza said. "We've been orphans a long time. I understand. I do. But they need to know. We're the same. I know it and you know it. And God—if he even fuckin' cares—knows it too. Me, Allan, and God, Goldie. We know. And I'll tell them."

"Move," Roger said.

"Don't touch me."

Marigold floated again on the invisible stretcher. Above the front door, the wind chime crooned. They put her in the SUV, the leather still warm from the day's sun.

"They don't love you." Eliza's voice was hollow, stretched-thin. "They say pretty things, but they aren't your mother. You and me, we're family. Blood. You were made in me. Wendy. Come and hug your mother. You forgive me, don't you? Our bond is eternal, it's—"

"Dad," Wendy said. "Take her home. Meet us at the hospital."

Roger wrapped his arms around Eliza.

"Now you wanna touch this brother-in-law fucker?"

He lifted and carried her to the car.

"Have 'em, Goldie. They're yours. But they aren't shiny up close. Their disappointment is yours now too."

"Get in the car," Roger said, straining.

"You'll never be a mother, Goldie. Doesn't matter what you give her, you'll never be her mother. And thank God for that. You were a useless daughter. A sinful wife. And you are a worthless sister."

The door slammed and her voice cut out.

Wendy ignored the rear-view camera and backed out into the street. As she drove, her gaze alternated from the road to her aunt, who laid supine, smiling. One of her bear slippers had fallen off and her foot was cold.

26

Marigold stood at the pool's edge, gripping the hearing aids like skipping stones. She cocked her arm.

They would understand.

Or they could destroy them together.

Hammer them to pieces. Burn them. Load them in a garlic masher and squeeze.

***

Inside was cool, empty. They had filled a shipping container with fragments of the house, the furniture packed together like bodies in a mass grave. Painter's tape lined the baseboards of Todd's room. On the canvas drop cloth were rollers, trays, and cans of unopened cobalt gray.

She climbed the stairs, the shiny brown of good leather shoes.

A double bed covered the carpet creases from where the racks of weights, floor mats, and treadmill had been.

In her bathroom, she opened the medicine cabinet and tossed the birth control packages— expiration dates 30 years past—into the trash. The back of the foil sheets were blown out like bullet holes. She covered them with toilet paper.

The phone rang.

"Today's the day." It was Betty. "Have you talked to Roger?"

"He's at my doorstep every morning like the newspaper."

"So he told you about Eliza?"

"He's been busy with the move."

"She's going back to her job at the rehab clinic."

". . ."

"You there?" Betty said.

"Yeah."

"I shouldn't tell you this, but I'm retiring so . . . But if you're not interested—"

"I'm listening."

"The divorce is uncontested."

Marigold moved the phone to her other ear. "I see."

"You figure out where they'll stay?"

"Guest rooms. Wendy doesn't want the master."

"That's nice."

"Yeah."

"Marigold."

"Present."

"You can talk to me."

"What do you think I'm doing? Anymore gossip?"

"Veronica terminated the pregnancy after finding out about—"

"Veronica?"

"Allan's step-daughter."

***

Roger and Wendy carried in his suitcases and crates of his stuff. They found pantry space for his grimy baking sheets, sacks of flour, and Mason jar of homemade yeast. In his closet, Marigold slipped his knotted neckties over the hook of a clothes hanger. It wasn't Monday, but they went grocery shopping all the same. Wendy paid.

***

Roger scrubbed the grill grates, while Wendy set up the outdoor speakers and skewered mushrooms, tomatoes, and chucks of bell pepper. Without permission, Marigold plucked Meyer lemons from a branch intruding into their yard. The smell of searing steaks and the rhythm of an acoustic guitar solo enchanted Roger. He clicked the kitchen tongs like castanets. Wendy smacked at his swishing apron and reminded him to flip the meat.

At the pool's ledge, Marigold poured glugging shots of whiskey and squeezed lemon juice, seeds and all, into three glasses of ice. Her feet stirred the pool water and her fingers stirred the drinks.

They ate. Salt and pepper sand coated the table. Strategically-placed citronella candles kept the insects at bay. They talked nonstop and argued jovially. After another round of whisky sours, they changed into their swimsuits and piled into the hot tub. The late afternoon sky darkened. Wendy snapped photos on her polaroid camera.

Roger drifted off to sleep, drifting on an electric orange raft, traversing the pool and bumping into the walls like a slow-moving pinball. His stomach hair glistened. Wendy tucked in patio chairs and harmonized with the R&B track coming from the speakers. They never did rent that karaoke machine. They never needed it.

The fibers of Marigold's mind coiled around the scene and ingested it into memory. Wendy stacked plates, shut the lid of the black-crusted grill, and completed the slipshod cleanup by licking a napkin and buffing out spots on the table of dried meat juice.

"Is there any left?" Wendy joined her aunt by the pool.

With her thumb and index finger, Marigold measured the amount of whisky left in the half-empty bottle. "I'm disappointed in us."

Wendy took it.

"Hang on. I'll borrow more lemons."

"Don't bother." Wendy drank it straight. She passed the whisky to her aunt.

Marigold took a sip. "That's enough of that." She sealed the bottle and cast it into the water. It floated toward Roger like a maritime delivery.

Wendy laughed. She kicked water toward her dad. The drops fell short and rippled the surface. She hummed along to the chorus of a song Marigold had never heard. "I talked to my mom."

"We can get a restraining order."

"I wanted to talk to her."

"Oh."

"She's moving near Mission Valley. It's a small place in an old building, but the bus stop out front will take her straight to work."

"That's good."

Wendy sang under her breath. Roger approached them. Together, they nudged him away, his ringless hand slipping into the water.

"Don't be mad."

Marigold looked at her niece. Beneath her white caftan beach cover up, she wore the swimsuit she had given her. "Have you ever seen me mad?"

"Mad?" She squeezed the water out from her braid. "Hmm."

Marigold smiled. "So what if I get mad?"

"I—we have so much, so . . . I gave mom money. Not a lot, but—"

"No, that's the . . . Christian thing to do."

"I sent some to your account too. So please don't think that—"

Marigold reached to cover Wendy's mouth. "Stop. We're family."

"Good." Wendy leaned back on her arms and exhaled. "Can we drink on it?"

"For you," Marigold descended into the water, "I'll risk electrocution." She turned away from her niece and paddled toward the bottle.

***

When summer ended, Roger returned to school in the Mustang. They bought a patio heater and set up croquet wickets on the front lawn, which the neighborhood kids came over from time to time to play with. Marigold attended improv classes, played with her new cell phone, and drove circuits at the cemetery. Pictures from backyard barbecues and weekend trips to Lake Arrowhead plastered the fridge.

27

The singer held the last note as the stage exploded with light. Roger stowed his wine glass between his legs and joined in the ovation. Below the TV, the fire burned feebly, more decoration than heat source. The show went to commercial, and Marigold lowered the volume.

Roger picked up What Happens at Night off the coffee table. "Any good?"

Marigold wanted to spoil what she knew of the plot so far and start an impromptu book club conversation right then and there. In the story a nameless couple travels days to a foreign country to adopt a baby. This is the wife's wish. Her dying wish. She's been made barren due to terminable cancer. What would Roger make of the premise? What did he think was the point of fulfilling this wish? But he asked if the book was good, not what it was about, so she just said, "I like it, but I can't get through it."

"That doesn't make sense."

"You know when you're reading and you go to turn the page but you can't? You lick your finger, but the page keeps slipping out. Do you think the book is trying to tell you something?"

He glanced at the TV, which advertised for life insurance. "Like what?"

"That you're not going to like what comes next. Or you missed something on that page."

"I think it means"—he explored the novel, careful to not let the bookmark fall out—"your motor skills are going—oh." The show's host introduced the next performer. "It's back on."

***

A taxi dropped off Wendy. She tracked them to the living room and kissed them sloppily on the cheeks.

Balled up in the recliner, Marigold draped the rainbow quilt over her knees. "Did you have fun?"

"Not compared to you two." Wendy picked through plates of olives and cheeses and reached for the empty wine bottle. She read the label, sounding out the French name. "But look." She scrolled through her phone. "Took a while, but you were right."

"You're swaying, dear. I can't see the screen."

"Take a seat." Roger took his feet off the couch. "Warmed it up for you."

Wendy sprawled out in front of the fireplace. "Ben's

going to visit."

"Ben?"

"I told him he can stay at my parent's house. You don't mind pretending, do you? I don't want to explain—"

"Whatever you want," Marigold said. "Be careful—you'll burn yourself."

Wendy tapped the glass between her and the flames. "Ow." She sucked on her finger. "It's hot."

"Astute as ever," Roger said.

"Hey." She crawled to the couch and hugged him. "I need to sleep."

He smiled. "And Ben needs to sleep down here."

Wendy pointed to Todd's old room. "He'll be our first guest."

"Deal."

"Alright. Good night, family."

It took three trips for Roger to clear the coffee table. While he washed the wine glasses, Marigold flipped through the channels. A newscaster tabulated the damage caused by the last fire season.

Roger squatted and combed through the rug for cracker crumbs. "It's funny." Despite their buzz, they had eaten neatly. The floor was spotless.

"Whaaa?" she said, yawning.

"Pretending to be her parents."

She muted the volume. "It's easier for everyone."

"I know, but . . ."

"But what?"

"Eliza was right."

"She's always right."

"She did say you'd steal her family."

"No, Rog. She said I could have you."

He stroked her hair. "You heard that?"

Marigold didn't respond.

"Let's make the family our own. How great would it be if Wendy had a brother or sister?"

"Stop." She gave him a playful push. "We'll wake her."

"She knows. And she'll be passed out. But if you're worried"—he squeezed her ear—"keep them in."

"If you keep your dentures in."

"These are my real—"

"Take your shower. I'll be in bed."

"Yes, mam." He saluted and jogged to the second floor.

The weatherman pranced in front of a blue map; temperatures dropped in every part of the country but theirs. She turned off the TV. The fake fire crackled on. Tomorrow was Saturday. They would sleep late and eat poached eggs on the patio in their pajamas. Maybe go for a swim.

Water surged through the pipes. No doubt Roger was rinsing his armpits, massaging a microbead cleanser into his skin, and smearing shaving cream over his stubble.

She'd brush her teeth for him.

She counted to three and kicked off the quilt. The door was locked, but she jiggled the handle anyway. She grabbed her book and, guided by the faint glow of the fireplace, made her way up the stairs.

ACKNOWLEDGMENTS

I want to thank the team at the Waterton Publishing Company for giving my short, absurd book a chance to get published. A huge shout-out goes to my friends; I look up to all of you. In particular, I'm grateful to Michael Conti for always being my first reader and such a demanding one at that. Our conversations always push me to explore new ideas about the world and myself. I also want to thank Darryl Leung for his impeccable taste and honest feedback while we workshopped sentences together. Of course, many thanks to my extended family on both the Carey and Walton sides. Special appreciation goes out to my mother Barbara Carey who gave me her love of reading and who always asks about and encourages my work. To my late father Dave Walton, whose vulnerable poetry is an inspiration. To my sisters Teri Lani and Maria Carey-Walton who did not influence this story's sibling dynamic at all—I'm so grateful every day for our close relationship. To my stepdad Daniel Harrington and mother-in-law Eunsun Kang who keep me full with love and food. To my brothers-in-law Keejung Son and William Chang for showing me that brotherly love I was missing. And a final thank you to every person, conversation, and interaction that has—consciously or otherwise—inspired this book.

STEVE CAREY-WALTON

Steve Carey-Walton grew up in San Francisco and studied journalism at San Diego State University. For the last ten years, he has lived in South Korea, where he works as a writer and editor. Where The Butterflies Sleep is his first book-length publication. His short stories have appeared in online literary journals.

www.ingramcontent.com/pod-product-compliance
Lightning Source LLC
Chambersburg PA
CBHW070341200726
48294CB00003B/738